DECEPTION BY DESIGN

DECEPTION BY DESIGN

TARA WENTZ

SAPPHIRE BOOKS

SALINAS, CALIFORNIA

Editor - Kaycee Hawn
Book Design- LJ Reynolds
Cover Design - Michelle Brodeur

Sapphire Books
Salinas, CA 93912
www.sapphirebooks.com

Printed in the United States of America
First edition – March 2015

This and other Sapphire Books titles can be found at
www.sapphirebooks.com

Dedication

To my dad, Larry—I only wish you were here to read this one as well. It's all the little things that made the difference… and I did notice!

~RIP~

Acknowledgments

First off, I would like to thank Sapphire Books for welcoming me into such a wonderful group. To Chris and Schileen for being publisher extraordinaires and also for your time and patience. Kaycee, my editor, you made the whole process very simple. Michelle Brodeur, for the cover even though I know you had some tough times to deal with during the process.

Thank you to all the people who helped me through this process because this book was a long time coming. I especially want to thank Terry, Tammy, Maya and Rai for their time and thoughts. Also, thank you to all the first round readers…I'm afraid to even try and name you all, but please know that I truly, truly appreciated everything!

At this time I have some very special thanks to dole out so please be patient because they really do need to be given.

Special Thanks:

Myra and LJ: You were my beta rocks! No matter how many times I asked or when I needed it you were there. Thank you doesn't seem like enough!

Michael Light: Your NASCAR knowledge and tickets made this whole process easier for even me to understand!

Toni Whitaker: For the IT and basketball knowledge.

Cari Hunter: Thank you for your medical expertise.

Tara Young: Your friendship and patience means the world!

Ms. Lyn St. James: First woman to win Rookie of the Year in the Indy 500 in 1992. Emailing with her gave me some great insight into the life of a female race car driver.

Last but not least, my family. Through thick and thin I know I can always count on them. My Mom: The strongest woman I know and I love her deeply. My brother, Wade and my sister, Candena: I know I can count on you. My son, Conner: I am so incredibly proud of the man you have become. My nieces and nephews: I have faith in anything and everything you want to be! Rhonda and Iny: Thank you for being such accepting aunts and embracing my family. Finally, to my love and life, Chris: Your love and support means more than you wiill ever know!

Please know that any inaccuracies within this story are my mistakes and mine alone.

Prologue

1...2...3...4 step and turn. 1...2...3...4 step and turn. 1...2...3...4 step and turn. The pacing back and forth kept up for hours and hours a day. The most recent picture was curled on the edges for having been in his hand day in and day out. The picture wasn't that old, but it had been some years since he'd seen her. He'd know that face anywhere, despite how different she looked.

She was smiling in the picture, but that wouldn't last for much longer. When he was done with her, she will have wished she had left well enough alone. People had learned in the past not to mess with him. An evil smile overtook his face at the thought of his last 'run-in.' As far as he was concerned that piece of shit deserved what they did to him! Hell, he didn't even have to pull the trigger himself.

He glanced back down at his hand, realizing that he had crumpled the picture in his anger. Anger was all he had to live by these days and that was all right with him. Once the right time came and business was taken care of, he'd disappear forever. Maybe, just maybe, then the anger would find a new home.

1...2...3...4 step and turn. 1...2...3...4 step and turn. 1...2...3...4 step and turn.

He uncurled the picture in his hand and spit on it. "I'm coming, bitch!"

Chapter One

Good afternoon race fans. Welcome to the I-70 Speedway here outside beautiful Kansas City, Missouri. It's a gorgeous day..."

Joshlyn Davis tuned out the announcer blaring in her ear and turned to frown at the woman next to her. "I can't believe I let you talk me into this."

"Oh, c'mon, Josh, you owed me. Besides, it's not that bad," her friend, Ami, stated.

Joshlyn rolled her eyes, turned back around, and continued down the stairs. Ami was the only person she had gotten close to in the two years she had lived in Kansas City. Thus being the only reason she was at this race, not to mention that Ami's brother happened to get them tickets because he was one of the drivers in today's race.

Finding their seats, they sat down and got comfortable. Joshlyn glanced around, taking in her surroundings. The stands were packed and the races were still a half hour from starting. Joshlyn had never been to the races before, mostly from lack of opportunity, but also because they had never really appealed to her. She could never understand how someone could get worked up about watching cars go around in circles. However, she did owe her friend since Ami went to the flea markets with her the previous weekend.

Joshlyn felt a nudge to her side and glanced back

to Ami. "What?"

"Are you still going to go down to the pit with me after the races?"

"I'm certainly not sticking around up here by myself," Joshlyn said, laughing.

"Great. I can't wait for you to meet Emerson. You are going to love him."

"Ahuh, so you keep telling me."

Ami grinned and propped her feet on the seat in front of her while she snacked on the bag of popcorn she had bought on the way to their seats. Shortly after Joshlyn moved to Kansas City, Ami started trying to set her up with her brother and each time Joshlyn had told her she just wasn't interested in dating. Finally, in a moment of startling clarity, only startling because it wasn't how she imagined it, Joshlyn blurted out that she was a lesbian. It's not that she was lying, just that she hadn't planned to tell Ami in quite that fashion. Since then, Ami had actively been looking for the perfect woman for her.

Joshlyn's thoughts meandered, but were interrupted when she realized Ami was talking to her again and she hadn't heard a word. "I'm sorry, what did you say?"

"Eventually you are going to have to relax and get out more. It's been two years since you moved here, Joshlyn, and I have yet to see you out with anyone."

How could Joshlyn tell her what those reasons were without giving away more details than she should? Ami's marriage was a fine example of true love, and although Ami was her friend, there were still things she just couldn't tell her.

"I'm content. I like where things are in my life. Why can't you be happy with that?"

Ami took her hand. "Oh, honey, I *am* happy for you. It's just that…" She stole a sidelong glance at Joshlyn before continuing. "I just want more for you, I guess. It's the romantic in me."

"I appreciate that," Joshlyn said, squeezing her hand. "Really, I do." She smiled at Ami and looked out over the track. "Enough of the deep stuff, tell me what to expect here."

"Okay. First, they will start by introducing the drivers. Once that's done, they will do the National Anthem. When the Anthem is done, the drivers will be instructed to start their engines; you following me so far?"

"Yep." Joshlyn nodded. "I gotcha, go on."

"Now, when that command is given you need to put those on," Ami said, motioning towards the headphones in Joshlyn's lap.

Joshlyn turned the headphones in her hand and then glanced at Ami. "It gets pretty loud, huh?"

"Oh, you have no idea. It will be so loud we probably won't even be able to talk."

"And you call that fun?" Joshlyn laughed.

"I know it doesn't sound like fun, but it really is more than just a bunch of cars going in circles."

"I'll take your word for it."

Ami grinned and bumped shoulders with Joshlyn. "You wait; you'll see."

"So why are there so many colored flags?"

"Ah, the flags themselves tell another story. Do you want the run down on all of them?"

"Sure, lay it on me."

"Okay. The race will start with the green flag. Green means go. The yellow flag means an accident has occurred on the track. It could also mean there is debris or some other kind of substance on the track."

"Do they stop the race if that happens?"

"No," Ami started, shaking her head. "All the cars get back around to the start or finish line, if you will, and then they line up behind the pace car. Once it's cleaned up and safe, the race will restart. The red flag is flown to stop the race. This can happen if there is bad weather or if the clean-up has to be done following a crash."

"So there are times when the race will be stopped."

"Right; well, under the right conditions, anyhow."

"Got it; please continue."

"The white flag means there is one lap to go and the black means a driver should proceed to the pits. Usually the black means there is a penalty towards a driver. Obviously you know what the checkered flag means…" Ami stopped briefly to let Joshlyn respond.

"That one I do know." Joshlyn laughed.

"The last two flags are known as the passing flag which is the blue one with the yellow slash through it and the red one with the X which means pit road is closed."

"Okay, I think I got it."

"Good, because there will be a quiz on it later." Ami chuckled.

Joshlyn grinned and shook her head. "Very funny!"

"*Race fans, momentarily we'll be introducing today's starting field. Our honorary starter today is CEO of Argus Construction, Lon Michaels.*"

"Here we go, doll." Ami stood and rubbed her hands together.

Joshlyn felt the spark of anticipation roll through the stands. She looked at the smiles, laughter, and overall happiness on the faces of the people around her. It was hard not to get caught up in all the excitement.

❧❧❧❧

Kellen Reynolds gulped down the last of her water and cracked open another bottle. There wasn't much longer before the race started so she wanted to hydrate as much as possible. This was going to be a little longer race than her previous couple and she wanted to be fully prepared. She spent time mentally priming herself and zoning her focus in on the goal she wanted to achieve. The goal was always the same; try to finish first. Mentally preparing was a key factor though and a step Kellen never skipped.

Her crew chief, Bob, had his head under the hood, looking things over one last time before they headed to the starting line. The guys made some adjustments that Kellen hoped would make a difference in today's run. She was centered and felt positive that this was going to be a great race.

"All right, kiddo, you ready to head that way?" Bob asked.

"Let's do it, Bob. I feel good today." Kellen swallowed down the last bit of water and threw the bottle in the recycle receptacle.

Bob chuckled and helped Kellen into the car. After she pulled her helmet on, he buckled the seat belt harness and made sure the strap was secure and tight.

"Go get 'em, tiger!"

Kellen tapped her fingers on the steering wheel as they made their way to the starting line. Once she fired up the engine, she knew the excitement and adrenaline would get her blood pumping. Oh, how she loved this sport!

❧❧❧❧

Joshlyn watched some of the race on the big screens along the side of the track. One car in particular kept her attention. The number thirteen car was making some great moves on the track and had moved up eight different times. She opened her program and flipped through the pages until she found the driver of the car. Immediately she was taken back with first that the driver was a woman, but secondly by how stunning she was. It was the eyes. She couldn't seem to look away from them. She read through every statistic and fact listed and then read it again.

"Hey, you're missing the race! What's got you so preoccupied?"

"I was just looking at information on some of the drivers." She closed the program and turned back to the race. She was watching, but the picture of Kellen Reynolds, the driver of car number thirteen, kept running through her mind. The race seemed to fly by and before Joshlyn knew it, the checkered flag was waving.

"Wow, I had no idea it could be that exciting."

Ami laughed outright at the exhilaration on Joshlyn's face. "You know, if I had any idea how much you would have enjoyed this, I would have talked you into it sooner."

Joshlyn grinned and nodded. She was a little

reserved at first, but it wasn't long before she was on the edge of her seat anticipating each move the drivers were making.

"Ready?" Ami asked, grabbing her stuff.

"Ready when you are," Joshlyn said. "Remember, no match making."

Ami shook her head and grabbed Joshlyn's hand. "Yeah, yeah, now come on."

Joshlyn followed her to the racing pits and watched as she enthusiastically hugged a tall, rugged-looking man that she could not have mistaken for anyone but Ami's brother. His shaggy, light blond hair and inviting smile were exact replicas of Ami's.

"Emerson, I'd like you to meet my good friend, Joshlyn. Joshlyn, this is my brother, Emerson."

Joshlyn stepped forward with her hand out only to have Emerson step back. Confused, she stepped back as well and glanced from sister to brother. Emerson had a crooked grin on his face.

"Sorry about that, Joshlyn. I was working on the car and have grease on my hands. I didn't want to get it all over you. Ami's used to it, but I didn't want to initiate you so fast." He rubbed his hands roughly with a towel but it would take more than that to get the grease off enough for a handshake.

Joshlyn smiled. "It's really nice to meet you, Emerson. I've heard a lot about you."

"It's nice to meet you, too." Emerson had been studying the attractive woman when they entered the pit area. She was taller than average, he guessed maybe five feet seven inches or so, and had a petite yet athletic looking figure. Her honey blonde hair hung in loose waves well past her shoulders.

"That was a great race, Em. Your car looked

good today."

"Thanks, Tater." Emerson grinned at Ami's scowl. He knew Ami really didn't mind his childhood nickname for her, but it was always fun to goad her into a response in front of her friends, just like big brothers were supposed to do regardless of the fact he was only seven minutes older. The nickname surfaced because for a time, the only thing Ami wanted to eat was mashed potatoes, French fries, or baked potatoes.

"She might have looked good, but she sure seems to be running a little rough." Emerson wiped his hands off one last time and tossed the rag on the hood of the car. "Did you ladies enjoy the race?"

"It was a lot of fun, as always," Ami proclaimed, giving Em a punch in the arm.

"Ouch, you brute!" Emerson teased while wrapping an arm around Ami's shoulders and squeezing.

Ami laughed but didn't pull away.

Emerson watched Joshlyn smile and visibly relax. "So, you guys want a little tour of the place?"

"That would be great." Ami glanced at Joshlyn for confirmation.

"Sounds good to me, too," Joshlyn agreed.

Emerson nodded towards the pit. "Well, c'mon then and I'll show you girls around."

Joshlyn listened intently while Emerson introduced them to some of the crewmembers and pointed out the various things around the pit. She glanced around at some of the other drivers and would have moved on except her eyes were drawn back to one driver in particular, Kellen Anne Reynolds. The woman was crouched down in front of a group of young girls who were nodding their heads. She talked and gestured with her hands, making the girls giggle.

Joshlyn smiled as one girl blushed when the woman patted her on the shoulder. It was easy to see the little girl was enamored with the striking woman. It was hard to tell how tall she was since she was still squatting, but the black driving suit hugged her body in all the right places, giving the impression of a sleek and well-toned physique. She had one side of her long dark hair pushed back behind her ear, and when she smiled, an even row of white teeth contrasted beautifully against her tan skin.

Based on the reactions from the girls, Joshlyn felt the driver had a good rapport with people or at least children, who, in her opinion, seemed to be great judges of character.

The girls said their goodbyes and the woman waved. Joshlyn hid a grin when the blushing girl turned back and hugged the slightly startled driver. She was somewhat curious when the woman placed a hand on the little girl's head, leaned down, and whispered in her ear. The girl grinned, nodded her head, and turned to catch up with her friends.

Joshlyn followed the girl's path until she was reunited with the others and then glanced back at the woman. She was unnerved to find those riveting eyes fixated on her. She stared back as the woman handed something to another driver and then walked in her direction. *Shit! She's coming this way.*

The closer the woman got, the more Joshlyn noticed the stark contrast between the woman's light colored eyes and her dark hair. The picture in the program did not do her justice.

Joshlyn was still staring as the woman smiled, showing a dimple on one cheek, and clapped Emerson on the shoulder.

"Great race, Emerson."

Emerson peered over his shoulder and turned. "Thanks, K. Hey, I'd like you to meet my sister, Ami, and her friend, Joshlyn. Ladies, this is Kellen Reynolds, one of the finest drivers I've ever had the pleasure to race against, even if she is a woman."

"Hey!" Kellen exclaimed. She shook hands first with Ami. "It's nice to finally meet you, Ami. I've seen you around before, but haven't had the pleasure of a formal introduction."

"It's nice to meet you as well, Kellen. You looked great today, too."

"Aw, thanks. It was a lot of fun out there." Kellen turned to Joshlyn and clasped her hand next.

Joshlyn tried to pull her gaze away from the blue eyes holding hers captive, but failed miserably. The longer she stood there with this woman's hand in hers, the more unsettled she felt. Very rarely did she meet someone that rattled her so quickly.

Joshlyn cleared her throat. "Hello. You really did look good."

Kellen quirked an eyebrow, but said nothing.

"Out there." Joshlyn thumbed towards the track and hurried to explain. "Racing."

"Thank you, I appreciate the compliment," Kellen responded in earnest.

Joshlyn held Kellen's gaze a moment longer before extracting her hand. She rubbed her hands together and turned to Ami.

"Um, are you about ready to go?"

Ami gave her a funny look at the abrupt comment, but nodded her head. "Uh, sure."

Joshlyn turned to Kellen. "It was nice to meet you."

"Likewise," Kellen said with a warm smile.

Joshlyn turned slowly away from Kellen and, finally breaking eye contact, she walked away from the drivers and the pit.

⁂

Kellen watched as the attractive blonde made her way across the pit area. *Wow, what a gorgeous woman!*

"She's a looker, huh?"

Kellen, almost forgetting that Emerson was still standing there, glanced up at him. She remembered his teasing comment about her being a woman and was going to harass him about it, but she knew all his teasing was in jest. He was a damn good driver and a fair one at that. "Yeah, what do you know about her?"

"I don't know anything about her."

At Kellen's raised eyebrow, Emerson responded, "Seriously, man. Ami hasn't said much other than she wanted me to meet her."

Kellen nodded in understanding and cuffed him on the shoulder again. "Well, I better get back over there," she said, gesturing towards her crew. "It was good seeing you again, Emerson. Take care."

"You, too, K; always a pleasure." Emerson gave a mock salute with two fingers and moved back towards his own crew.

As Kellen walked back over to her area, she couldn't stop thinking about Joshlyn and her warm brown eyes. They captivated Kellen completely. She wondered what her story was and why she seemed so standoffish. "Maybe she's just shy," Kellen mumbled. "There is a lot of testosterone to take in down here." She glanced around and sighed. There weren't many women Kellen dated that could handle all the grease and noise either so what was she expecting? Not that she made much effort to date anymore. It seemed easier to just go about her daily business and continue the focus on her driving.

❧❧❧❧

Joshlyn waved goodnight to Ami, closed the front door, and punched in the code to reactivate the home alarm system. Laying her jacket over the chair, she tossed her keys on the foyer table and kicked off her shoes. She glanced around the room, taking in the various pieces of furniture and sparse decorations. This should have felt like home, but Joshlyn doubted it ever would.

"Even with the lights on it still feels so dark in here," she said with a sigh.

She tapped her fingers lightly against the table and reflected back on the day at the races. It really was a lot more fun than she had expected. What was more surprising was the way she reacted towards Kellen. She had lived in Kansas City long enough to have met plenty of people, but never had she felt the need or desire to really get to know someone. She couldn't remember the last time she'd had that type of feelings towards anyone. She wanted to get to know Kellen better, yet the thought of it scared her into running. Ami hadn't asked a lot of questions on the drive home, but Joshlyn knew they were in the back of her mind.

Joshlyn wandered down the hall to her bedroom, turning lights off as she went. She unbuttoned her shirt and, pulling a clean T-shirt and panties out of the dresser, she looked nervously to the windows, a habit born out of necessity to assure her that the blinds were closed and nobody could see in. She rubbed the scar near her shoulder, sighed, and sat heavily on the bed, tossing her clothing aside. She hesitated briefly before she opened the drawer on her nightstand and removed an old wooden box. Running her hand lightly across the top, she carefully lifted the lid. Her eyes scanned the contents of the box, but she couldn't bring herself to touch them. Closing her eyes, she massaged her temple with the fingers on her left hand.

"God, when will I ever get past this? Does it ever get easier?"

She opened her eyes, closed the lid on the box, and placed it back in the drawer. Frustrated, Joshlyn slammed the drawer shut, grabbed her clothes, and headed to the bathroom to get ready for bed.

❧❧❧❧

Kellen held a long past warm beer in her hand while gazing up into the dark sky. She could see a few errant clouds lit up by the bright half moon and lots of twinkling stars. Most of her crew had already called it a night, but she and her crew chief, Bob, remained lounging in their chairs.

"Bob, do you ever wonder why some people grab your interest more than others?"

"I quit thinking about that long before my third wife left. Figured it just wasn't in the cards for me."

Bob had been her crew chief for the entire four years she'd been driving for this group, but she'd known him a lot longer. Bob was the brother of Mason, who was one of her grandfather's best friends. Mason took her under his wing after her grandfather passed away so she'd seen Bob around here and there. Mason was the one that got Kellen into driving in the first place. It wasn't until after Mason died that Bob approached her with an offer to keep driving and ultimately put her in the position she was in today. He was a great guy, but never struck her as the family type. Racing and cars were his wife and kids.

Bob took a swig of beer then asked, "What makes you ask a question like that anyhow?"

Kellen shrugged and remained silent for a bit. "I don't know. Sometimes I just get a little introspective. I start wondering if this," she waved her hand around her, indicating the track and cars, "is all there is; will I find that special person to spend my life with or not. You know?"

"Kellen, she's out there, just give it time." Bob paused, thinking. "You're what, twenty-eight?"

"Twenty-nine and soon to be thirty."

"See? Plenty of time. Quit thinking about it so much. It's not like you haven't gone out on dates or had a lack of company."

"Yeah, I suppose."

Kellen knew exactly why she had asked Bob this question. Joshlyn had been on her mind since the moment she'd left the pit area. The woman was beautiful in a down-to-earth, girl-next-door kind of way. She was wholesome looking to a fault. Her peaches and cream complexion made Kellen's fingers beg to caress it. She'd had sexual responses to women before, but this was more. It wasn't just a sexual longing.

Kellen took a sip of beer and set it down. "Blech, that's nasty." Standing, she nudged Bob's shoulder. "I'll see you later. Don't stay too late."

"See ya later, kiddo. You did good today."

"Thanks," she said with a grin.

Bob's praises always meant a lot because he didn't give them away freely. He was more of a father figure than she'd ever had. Her own father had never acknowledged that she existed, much less to be around for any of her accomplishments. He was a drunk and cared only about himself. Last she'd heard, he was doing time in prison.

Kellen walked past Emerson's pit area and stopped. Backtracking, she poked her head around the corner and saw Emerson and a couple of his crewmembers.

"Hey, Emerson…guys," she said with a nod, acknowledging the others.

Emerson glanced at his watch then back at Kellen. "You're here kind of late."

"Yeah, one of the perks of being your own boss; you get to make your own hours. I get to start my day whenever I want."

Laughing, Emerson said, "Then that makes you one lucky gal. You on your way out?"

She nodded then waited while Emerson said goodnight to his crew. Most of the drivers seemed to hang out awhile after the race, letting the adrenaline rush work its way out of their systems.

As they walked towards the parking lot, Kellen fidgeted with her keys nervously. She took a deep breath and blew it out. "Um, are you going to the Pit barbeque next weekend?"

Emerson grinned, watching as Kellen looked everywhere but at him.

Kellen felt irritated with her nervous behavior. It was so out of character for her. She always wanted to give off the impression of self-assuredness and confidence.

He cleared his throat before answering. "I had planned on it. How about you?"

"Same here. Do you, uh, think your sister will be coming?"

"I'll see if she's busy and ask her. Want me to see if she'd like to bring Joshlyn along?"

Kellen grinned shyly. "That would be great, Emerson. Thanks."

Emerson nudged her with his elbow. "No problem. Listen, I'll talk to you later, K."

"Good night."

Kellen drove home thinking about the Pit barbeque and how much fun they usually were. It was a time when the drivers, including friends and family, could get together and mingle. Although she enjoyed herself, she always felt like something was missing. She attended out of an obligation, but this year she wondered if it would be different.

Chapter Two

Kellen scooted her chair away from the desk and leaned back. She reached under her glasses to rub her tired eyes with the pads of her fingers. Sighing, she steepled her fingers under her chin and gazed at the computer screen. How many days and nights had she sat in this same spot working for hours without a single thought except for the program on which she was working? This was definitely the best part about being your own boss. The list of jobs she routinely did or could do was a mile long. Between software development and graphic art design, she was constantly busy. She rarely turned a job away. Kellen loved the challenge and diversity of each job and even had some contracts for ongoing support.

She reached for the ringing phone that had interrupted her thoughts. "KR Design and Development."

"Hey, Kellen, it's Lance Bowman with OSM. I was wondering if you had time to drop by this week. We've got some new forms that need to be dropped into the system."

Kellen had been working with OSM for over a year now. They did medical exams for life insurance policies as well as disability and long-term care policies. She had developed a cataloging system for the different insurance companies and various medical forms that were used.

"Sure, Lance, that won't be a problem. How about..." She trailed off while shuffling through her appointment book. "Here we go, how about Wednesday? I have anything from nine until eleven-thirty open."

"Sounds great, how about nine? Oh, and can you bring some sample copies of those brochures you designed? I think we're about ready to venture into that avenue," he said rather proudly.

"You got it. See you then." Kellen hung up the phone after his goodbye and chuckled. She had been trying to convince him for six months that the flyers, at a minimum, would improve business.

Kellen stretched her arms above her head and arched her back. Hearing it pop, she gracefully stood and decided it was time for some lunch.

"C'mon, Chigger. Let's go grab something to eat," Kellen said, watching her Welsh Corgi stand and stretch. He liked to lay by her feet near the computer tower because of the heat the fans generated. It didn't matter what time of year it was, Chigger loved the heat.

She walked through the living room and flipped the switch on the stereo as she walked past. An upbeat rock song blared through the speakers as she danced her way into the kitchen.

☙ ☙ ☙ ☙

Joshlyn clipped the last group of pictures to her dry line and stepped back. She never liked to stack her photos after printing them for fear the ink would smear or smudge. The dry line gave the prints time to dry while also affording her the opportunity to study them without touching them. There were plenty of pictures to submit this time around and Joshlyn knew Ami wouldn't be disappointed in the quality either. Ami was her direct contact with a firm that used her photos. She glanced across her large L-shaped desk and smiled. It had turned out nice and she loved the large working space. She wondered sometimes if she would have been as involved with photography had she not been forced to choose another career path. Photography was something she enjoyed, but always considered a hobby up until three years ago.

Joshlyn shook her head, ridding herself of the unwanted thoughts. Thinking of the past always left her stomach feeling a little queasy. She pulled off her gloves, cleaned up the mess on her desk, and then moved to look at the prints prior to the ones she had just finished. There was a mixture of scenic and animal prints. She stopped at one picture in particular.

"Wow, that turned out really nice." It was a black and white of a baby bird hatching. The little beak barely protruded through the shell as it worked its way out. After spotting the nest and climbing part way up the tree, Joshlyn couldn't believe her luck at capturing the event through the entire sequence. She snapped several frames before lowering the camera and watching the joy of nature at its best.

Joshlyn glanced at her watch and placed the dried prints in an envelope. She had just enough time to get cleaned up and eat before Ami came to collect the photos.

❧ ❧ ❧ ❧

Ami glanced through the photographs one last

time before looking up into Joshlyn's anxious eyes. After three years, Joshlyn was still nervous about sharing her photographic results.

"These are really good, Josh," Ami said, knowing they would be whether she looked at them or not.

"Thanks," Joshlyn said with a wide smile.

"You outdid yourself with these, my friend." Ami laughed outright at Joshlyn's blush. "C'mon, don't tell me you don't know how good you are."

"Stop it, Ami. Why is it that you like to pick at me so much?" Joshlyn asked, not really expecting an answer.

Ami patted her knee, but continued to smile. "Listen, Emerson called and asked if we were interested in going to the Pit barbeque this Saturday. He specifically asked that I invite you. Interested?"

"Um, I don't know. Are you going to go?" Joshlyn knew that since Ami's husband, Jaxon, was out of town on business a lot, chances are he wouldn't be able to make it and she also knew Ami didn't really like to go out and do things on her own.

"I think it will be fun. I've been before and enjoyed the people and the great food. It's a very laid back, relaxed atmosphere."

Joshlyn chewed nervously at her bottom lip and glanced down at her hands.

"Joshlyn, it's no big deal if you don't want to go."

"It's not that I don't want to go. It's just that…" Joshlyn hesitated, wishing she could explain. *I hate this!*

"Okay, how about if we go and at any point you feel you need to leave, then just say so and we'll go, no questions asked."

Joshlyn knew Ami was always true to her word

so she reluctantly agreed.

"Okay," she said, nodding.

"Great," Ami exclaimed, clapping her hands together. "I promise you'll have a good time."

Joshlyn couldn't help but smile at Ami's excitement. Maybe this really was what she needed

Ami stood, grabbing the envelope of pictures. "Well, I better get these turned in before they come hunting me down."

Joshlyn walked her to the door. "What time do I need to be ready Saturday?"

"I'll come get you about 2:30, so be ready."

"Do I need to bring anything?"

"Nope, I got it covered. Dress comfortable though," Ami said as she stepped out the door and onto the porch.

"Comfortable I can do. And Ami," she waited until Ami looked at her. "Thanks."

Ami patted her cheek lightly and smiled. "You're welcome, sweetie. For future reference, I'm here if you ever want to talk about what's on your mind."

Joshlyn closed the door and blew a breath out. She leaned against the door for a minute before walking over and plopping down on the couch. There wasn't anything more that she wanted other than to feel accepted and give life a chance for once. Maybe this was her opening. Maybe she could let her guard down just a little…maybe…She could remember as plain as if it were yesterday the last time she had gotten together with anyone. Her family was not large by any means, but all her parents' friends and co-workers had always been an unquestioned extension. Joshlyn was the youngest of three girls. She was also shy, quiet, and reserved, which infuriated her sisters because she always drew the attention of the eligible men that attended the functions. Her oldest sister constantly belittled her. They had many an argument, but on this last get together, she went way beyond just belittling.

"Why do you even attend these functions? You know you don't like them and all you do is attract all the attention to yourself!"

"Heather, I have no idea what you are talking about. I can't help that they all talk to me. I do nothing to encourage them."

"Don't you see, little sister, that that is exactly what they like? Why can't you be loud and obnoxious? Why can't you, just for once, try and make things a little easier for the rest of us?"

"I don't understand you, Heather. I'm damned if I do and damned if I don't!"

Joshlyn remembered that her sister just got madder and madder and talking to her was of no use. She'd had enough of the shenanigans and decided it was better just to turn in for the night.

"This is solving nothing, Heather. I'm calling it a night." As she turned to go, Heather grabbed her arm and jerked her back around.

"Oh no, this is far from over. Tonight we are getting to the bottom of this!" Heather hollered.

"Let go of me, Heather, I mean it."

"Or what, huh?"

Before she could say or do anything else, her other sister came into the room. "What is going on? We can hear you two yelling clear out on the veranda."

Heather and Diane were closer in age and definitely closer overall. There was no way Diane was coming to her rescue despite the fact that Heather was bigger and stronger.

Heather turned to look at Diane and smirked. "I'm finally getting little miss goodie two shoes here to talk."

Diane grinned, but didn't say a word.

"I'm done with this, Heather. Let me go."

"No way, sister dear."

Joshlyn could still feel how Heather's hands felt on her. She rubbed her palms lightly up and down her arms as if she could vanquish the thoughts, but continued to think back on that night.

Heather shoved her down on the couch and held her with a hand on each shoulder. "No more, little sister. From here out you will make your excuses to Mother and bow out of future gatherings. Do you understand?"

"I will not disappoint Mother, not even for you, Heather."

"Of course you wouldn't! Mother's little darling! I mean it!"

"No, Heather."

Heather looked at Diane and then back before raising a hand and slapping her in the face. "You'll do it or so help me you'll regret it!" She slapped her over and over until her lip was split and her eye was starting to bruise. "Say it! Say you'll do it!"

"No!"

Heather drew back her arm to hit her again when it was grabbed from behind. Their father had stopped the beating and jerked Heather off the couch.

"What in God's name are you doing?" He bellowed.

"She started this, Father!"

"I don't know what has gotten in to you girls, but I will not have this evening spoiled by your bickering and carrying on, do you hear me?"

"But Father—" Heather started.
"Enough!"
That night was the final straw for all of them. Joshlyn's father turned to leave and stumbled into a table. He turned, grabbed his chest, and dropped to the ground. Her mother rushed in and all hell broke loose. After everything was settled and the funeral was over, her mother wanted to know what happened. Heather and Diane threw her under the bus and made it all her fault. Her mother still didn't give the girls her full attention until the next gathering. Not wanting another scene, Joshlyn begged out of the festivities. When her mother kept badgering and telling her she'd never find a man if she didn't put herself out there, she finally admitted to her that she was gay and was not looking for a man. After that point, her sisters had their mother's attention all to themselves.

Joshlyn was nervous, but ready. It was time to put herself out there…even if just a little bit.

❧ ❧ ❧ ❧

Kellen stood in front of the closet with a smile on her face. The week had flown by and she'd been very productive. Lance was pleased with the brochure designs that she had presented him on Wednesday and wanted to move forward with them. She was also working on a support system for a new dry cleaning and laundry service that opened up just down the street. One of their customers had referred them to Kellen, saying how pleased they were with her services. The initial meeting ran very smoothly and they were happy with the ideas she had presented. They cut her a check for the deposit that very day. *Yep, things were indeed picking up.*

Kellen contemplated what shirt to wear before turning away from the closet in disgust.

"Now if only getting dressed were as easy," she mumbled to the empty room. "Why does this have to be so difficult? It's just a damned barbeque."

She ran her fingers through her hair and yanked a dresser drawer open. Grabbing a light blue T-shirt, she pulled it over her head and tucked it loosely into her navy athletic shorts.

Kellen sat on the edge of the bed and slipped on sneakers rather than sandals. There were usually a couple of basketball games going on throughout the day and she loved shooting hoops. It was always amazing how much camaraderie there was off the track considering that on the track it was every man for himself. There was a brotherhood among the drivers and Kellen was very pleased to be included within those ranks. A low whine brought her thoughts from the track to the side of her bed.

Chigger stared at her, begging to be helped onto the bed. He had no problems getting off the bed, but getting on was another story. Kellen wondered more often than not if it was because he was just lazy.

Laughing, Kellen bent down. "Chigger, one of these days you're gonna have to figure this out for yourself. I can't keep lifting you on this bed, you big chicken!"

Chigger barked at her and stamped his paws playfully. She lifted him to the bed and watched as he walked in circles before dropping down and looking at her.

"Why do you find it necessary to plop your fat little ass right on my pillow, hmm?"

Chigger laid his head on his paws and closed his eyes, ignoring her. Kellen leaned down on one elbow and scratched him lightly behind the ears. Three years ago, she had picked him up from a local animal shelter and he'd been her steady companion since. He apparently had been rescued from an old man that had abused him on a regular basis. If Kellen raised her voice at all, the poor dog would scramble under the bed and hide or leave the room all together. Over the last year, his blonde fur had turned white in several places.

She fingered the triangular shaped scar on his head. "Well boy, I better get a move on if I'm gonna get there on time." She ran her hand down his back and patted his rump lightly before standing.

Kellen grabbed her keys and headed for the door, stopping briefly to grab the sweatshirt she had set out. The days were warm, but she didn't want to be unprepared because the nighttime was generally on the cool side.

❦ ❦ ❦ ❦

Joshlyn ran her hand across the mirror to wipe off the condensation and wondered how long it would take for her to grow accustomed to the eyes staring back at her. Three years was long enough; she should be used to it by now. She tried not to dwell on things she could not change, like the looks on the faces of people she thought were her friends, but sometimes it got the better of her. She shook her head, refusing to allow herself to be taken back down memory lane.

"I've got a barbeque to get ready for and tonight I'm going to relax and enjoy myself."

Joshlyn tossed her towel aside and entered her bedroom. She slipped into her red polo and khaki shorts, wondering if Kellen was going to be there. She hoped the intriguing woman was there even though the thought of seeing her was terrifying. It had been a long time since she'd felt even an inkling of desire for anyone. *Why now?*

She buckled her belt and hurried into her topsider tennis shoes, knowing that Ami would be arriving soon. She sprayed some of her favorite cologne on and smiled. The fresh clean scent always made her feel energized. She took one last look in the mirror, flipped the light switch off, and headed down the hall.

Joshlyn checked the locks on the back door and the kitchen windows. A glance out the window confirmed that the honk from a car horn was Ami. Grabbing her sweater, sunglasses, and keys, Joshlyn took one last look around the living room and examined every detail. Satisfied, she stepped out and closed the door behind her.

Chapter Three

Kellen bent over, hands tugging at the bottom of her shorts, trying to catch her breath. She and some of the others at the barbeque had been playing basketball for about an hour now. Kellen overtly watched Joshlyn as the day progressed. They ran into each other a couple of times and were courteous, but Kellen wasn't sure Joshlyn wanted more contact than a general hello. Joshlyn was hard to read and Kellen didn't want to push her luck. Although, there were several times she had caught Joshlyn looking her way only to pretend interest in something else when spotted.

"Heads up, K."

Kellen turned her head just as a ball came flying her way. Catching it with ease, she strolled back over to the group of players.

Emerson gestured towards her and asked, "You up for a game of one on one?"

"Ready when you are."

"Ahuh, sure you are." He smirked.

Kellen rolled her eyes, knowing that Emerson was more than aware he hadn't had her full attention. She pulled her shoulders back and fired the ball into Emerson's waiting hands. "Bring it on, hot shot."

Kellen squared up, waiting for Emerson to take the ball out at mid-court. Slowly he dribbled inbounds, making his way towards the basket. He crossed from one side to the other with Kellen matching him step for step. Realizing he wasn't going to shake her, Emerson lowered his shoulder and drove to the basket. After a few steps, he stopped abruptly and pulled up for a jump shot. Kellen managed to get the tips of her fingers on the ball as it left his hands, causing the ball to bounce around the rim before dropping in.

"Lucky shot."

"Lucky? That was a damn good shot with you in my face, Reynolds."

"Nah, if I'd been in your face, you'd never have gotten the ball off." Kellen grinned.

"Whatever! Just take the damn ball out."

"Let me show ya how it's really done."

"All talk, K. That's all you are," Emerson taunted.

Kellen bounced the ball several times before crossing half court and making her way to the baseline. She'd only taken two steps before pulling up and letting the ball fly from outside the three-point arc.

Swish.

"Nothing but net, my friend."

Emerson grabbed the ball and mumbled on his way back to the line. "I wasn't ready, that's all."

"I can do it all day long, baby, all day long," Kellen said, laughing.

❧ ❧ ❧ ❧

Dribbling down the lane, Emerson had his back to Kellen, trying to muscle in further. The basket loomed closer and Emerson set his feet, ready to make his move. He faked one direction then turned back for what should have been an easy hook shot. However, Emerson didn't anticipate Kellen being in his face as he turned. Arms bent slightly at the elbow, ball in outstretched hands, he swung around and caught Kellen in the side of the head with an elbow. In slow motion, he watched her eyes widen in surprise before they rolled up and closed as she dropped to the ground.

"Shit," Emerson exclaimed, letting the ball drop from his hands.

๑ ๑ ๑ ๑

The barbeque had been in full swing for a couple hours and there were various activities going on. Joshlyn sat munching on potato chips while perusing the different groups of people visiting or playing games. She sat half-listening as Ami carried on a conversation with a couple of women she had been introduced to earlier. Joshlyn was well aware of Kellen's actions and her whereabouts throughout the day. Glancing at the basketball court, she noticed Kellen and Emerson were the only ones playing now. Joshlyn smiled when she saw Kellen laughing at something Emerson said. Joshlyn followed her strong calves and toned thigh muscles that led up to a trim waist. She caught a glimpse of Kellen's flat abdomen when Kellen brought her arms up to defend the ball. Joshlyn bit her bottom lip as she watched Kellen's breasts strain against her T-shirt. Shaking her head slightly, Joshlyn continued to study Kellen's body, making her way up to a soft sensuous neck that begged to be kissed and nuzzled.

Good God, Joshlyn! What the hell's the matter with you? It's not like you've never seen a woman before!

Joshlyn was shocked when her gaze collided with blue eyes that she was sure were laughing at her for being caught staring. Joshlyn smiled and turned her head, pretending to listen as Ami continued an animated conversation with the girls.

Just my luck that she'd catch me.

Joshlyn rubbed her forehead in frustration, catching Ami's attention in the process.

"Hey," Ami asked, placing a hand lightly on Joshlyn's arm. "You doing okay?"

"Yeah, I'm fine." When Ami looked unconvinced, Joshlyn rushed to reassure her. "Really, I'm fine."

"Be sure and let me know when you're ready to go."

"I will. I'm having a good time. You were right about me needing to get out."

"Really? You don't say?" Ami said with a smirk.

"Oh, stop that! Don't push your luck." Joshlyn grinned at her before continuing, "You have a nice group of friends here."

"Yeah, some are nicer than others, huh?" Ami teased as Joshlyn glanced at the basketball court yet again.

A distracted Joshlyn barely replied, "Ahuh."

"Josh?" Ami waited with no reply. "Joshlyn."

"What?" Joshlyn asked, snapping back to the conversation. She immediately blushed when she saw the smile Ami was trying to hide.

"Gorgeous, huh?" Ami asked, gesturing to the court.

"Yes, she is and very good at basketball, too."

Ami nodded her head. "Ahuh, that she is."

"Do you know much about her?" Joshlyn asked.

"What exactly would you…oh my God!" Ami jumped to her feet and ran towards the basketball court.

Joshlyn jumped at the startled exclamation and looked over to the court where Ami was running. She barely caught sight of a dark head of hair as she watched the person drop to the ground. Looking back up, she realized it was Kellen and took off for the court herself.

❧❧❧❧

"Back up people. Give her some room."

Emerson knelt on the ground next to Kellen. He put a hand on her shoulder to restrain her from getting up.

"Hey, take it easy, K."

"I'm fine, let me up," Kellen said, slapping at his hands and trying to sit up.

"Kellen!"

At Emerson's raised voice, Kellen quit fighting and lay back down.

Emerson softened his voice before continuing. "Please, just stay still and let me make sure you're okay."

Aside from racing cars, Emerson was a paramedic. Years of training kicked in as he slowly, but precisely assessed Kellen's condition.

After assuring himself that Kellen was not having any problems other than a large bump forming on the side of her head, Emerson sat back on his haunches.

"You've got a pretty nasty bump here, K. It's probably nothing to be concerned about, but you may have a mild concussion. You weren't out but just a few seconds, if that."

"I'm sure it's nothing." Emerson's look of uncertainty made her continue. "Seriously; except for the headache, I feel fine."

"Listen, I'm really sorry about this—"

"Don't be," Kellen interrupted. "It was an accident."

Emerson nodded his head in understanding. "You ready to sit up?"

Kellen glanced at the crowd that had gathered around them. She hated being the center of attention, especially when she wasn't at her best. It left her feeling extremely vulnerable. She nodded, and then swallowed at the nausea the motion caused.

"Take it slow," Emerson said, helping her to a sitting position. "Okay?"

"So far, so good."

Kellen patted his knee then took his hand to stand. Emerson wrapped an arm around her waist and helped her to her feet. Once there, Kellen's legs felt like rubber. She wasn't sure they would hold her until another warm pair of hands grasped her other arm. She looked into Joshlyn's concerned eyes and smiled. Images swam in front of Kellen's eyes as she swayed unsteadily on her feet.

"Whoa." Emerson tightened his arm around her waist.

Kellen blinked her eyes a couple times and took a breath. "I'm okay, Emerson. Thanks."

"All right. Well, I think you should head on home and get out of this heat. You need to take it easy for a while and put some ice on that bump."

"Yes, Daddy," Kellen said, smirking.

Emerson scowled at her for a second before adding, "You also shouldn't be driving." Emerson put his hand up when Kellen rolled her eyes. "I'm serious, Kellen."

Joshlyn watched the interaction between the two before stepping forward.

"I can take you home, Kellen. I rode with Ami so I could drive your car, and I'm sure Ami wouldn't mind picking me up later."

Kellen's heart raced at the thought of spending some alone time with Joshlyn.

"All..." Kellen cleared her throat. "All right, if you're sure you don't mind."

Joshlyn glanced at Ami with a raised eyebrow. Seeing her nod, she said, "It's no problem at all."

Kellen tipped her head in acknowledgement.

Ami moved closer and placed a hand on Joshlyn's arm. "You sure you're okay with this?"

Joshlyn glanced at Kellen and then back to Ami. "I'm sure. We'll be fine."

Ami studied her for a moment before nodding. "All right, call me later and I'll get directions to pick you up."

"Will do."

By this time, the crowd had dispersed and gone about their business. Joshlyn and Kellen made their way over to where Kellen's things were sitting. Joshlyn grabbed them, turned and waved goodbye to Emerson and Ami, and led Kellen to the parking lot.

"Where are you parked?"

"Just up ahead here. You sure you don't mind?"

Joshlyn kept pace with Kellen and smiled. "I'm sure. Why? Are you having second thoughts about me driving your car?"

"No. Not at all," Kellen rushed to assure her.

"Ahuh, give me the keys, Sport."

Kellen grumbled good-naturedly, but handed the keys to her. "I'm right here."

Joshlyn eyed the sparkling, metallic blue Endeavor appreciatively. "Oh, nice." She unlocked the passenger door and waited while Kellen got in safely before going around to the driver's side.

Joshlyn adjusted the seat and pulled the seat belt across her to buckle it. Out of her peripheral vision, she could see that Kellen was looking in her direction. She glanced up, catching the heat in Kellen's gaze.

Kellen couldn't help but notice the assuredness with which Joshlyn performed each task as she prepared to drive them home. It was so different from the somewhat timid Joshlyn that Kellen had observed so far. She watched long, slender fingers as they moved about, adjusting everything. Kellen could smell the clean fragrance of Joshlyn's cologne as she leaned her direction to buckle her seat belt. The close proximity of Joshlyn lit a fire inside Kellen's body. Warm brown eyes captured her own a moment too soon. Kellen looked away and fastened her own seat belt.

Joshlyn cleared her throat. "So, which way?"

Kellen gave her brief instructions and she put the vehicle in gear to pull out of the parking lot. Kellen's presence was distracting, making it very difficult for her to focus. She could feel Kellen's eyes on her, making her mind buzz with curiosity. *What is she looking at? What is she thinking? Say something, Joshlyn!*

"What do you do when you're not racing cars?" Joshlyn asked, without taking her eyes off the road.

Kellen was resting back against the headrest, but had her head rolled in Joshlyn's direction. "I run a business out of my home."

The low drawl that Kellen spoke with awoke an ache in Joshlyn that she thought was long gone. She took a deep breath and caught the scent of sweat and soap.

"What type of business is it?"

"Mostly graphic and software design, but a little bit of IT stuff as it pertains to my software programs."

"That sounds interesting. Does it keep you busy?"

"I like it and yeah, it has been busier as of late."

"That's always a good thing," Joshlyn said, glancing at her briefly and smiling before turning her eyes back to the road.

Kellen smiled in return, knowing that Joshlyn couldn't see it, but not really caring. She couldn't seem to take her eyes off of Joshlyn. When they first got into the vehicle, Kellen noticed a sheen of moisture along Joshlyn's hairline. The longer they drove the more it faded as the air conditioner took over. *Kellen, you are in trouble!*

Joshlyn followed Kellen's directions to her house with no problem. She lived in a quiet, older neighborhood with large trees lining the streets. She pulled into the driveway Kellen indicated and glanced at the house and yard. The house was a light gray bungalow with white trim. The meticulous lawn was plush and green. Joshlyn itched to take her shoes off and walk barefoot through it.

"You can pull on around back. I usually go in that way."

As Joshlyn pulled around back, Kellen hit the remote, opening one side of the two car detached garage. After parking, Joshlyn handed Kellen her keys back after they walked out of the garage. The back yard was large in comparison to the front and had a privacy fence surrounding it. While waiting for Kellen to close and latch the gate, Joshlyn looked around the yard. The lot had several trees providing shade over most of the yard. Between two trees, a large hammock swung lightly in the miniscule breeze. Off the back of the house was a good-sized wooden deck, which was beautifully stained in a rich redwood. A patio set complete with umbrella sat in one corner while a grill and smoker sat in the other.

"C'mon in."

Joshlyn followed Kellen up the two short steps of the deck to the sliding glass doors. "This deck is beautiful."

Kellen hesitated only briefly, but it was long enough for Joshlyn to see the pain that flickered in her eyes. "Thank you. It took a whole summer to do, but it was more than worth it."

Joshlyn was astonished. "You did this all by yourself?"

"Um, yeah, I did." Kellen opened the sliding doors and entered the kitchen with Joshlyn following. Joshlyn recognized when a topic was closed for discussion and this was definitely one of those topics.

Joshlyn only managed a couple steps into the house when a small, but well-fed dog approached her.

"This is Chigger," Kellen said, squatting slowly to pet him. "He won't bite. He's afraid of his own shadow."

Joshlyn chuckled and bent down to pet the dog whose wagging tail made his whole body wiggle.

"He's cute. What breed of dog is he?"

"A Welsh Corgi. I got him three years ago from the shelter. He's been a great companion and doesn't complain...much," Kellen added while watching Chigger's antics.

Kellen grinned as she watched the silly dog turn into a puddle under Joshlyn's ministrations. She also took notice of the fine muscle tone of Joshlyn's thighs. The lightly tanned skin looked so soft. Kellen watched the muscles flex in Joshlyn's forearm as she reached up to push a lock of hair behind her ear. A small ear displayed a single diamond stud that twinkled in the light. Kellen followed Joshlyn's slender neck down to the open collar of her shirt. She knew if she leaned forward just a little, she'd probably be able to see right down Joshlyn's shirt.

Flustered, Kellen turned towards the cabinet to get a glass down.

"Would you like something to drink?"

Joshlyn jumped back to her feet and moved in next to Kellen, placing a hand on the small of her back. "Hey, why don't you let me get that?"

Kellen pulled her hand back at the same time Joshlyn reached for the glass. The slight brush of Joshlyn's hand against hers sent a warm sensation down her spine. "I can get it."

"I know you can, but humor me, will you?"

Kellen acquiesced and stepped back.

Joshlyn smiled sympathetically and asked, "What would you like?"

"Water would be fine, thanks," Kellen responded, knowing that Joshlyn had no idea what prompted her flustered reply and probably mistook it for the head injury.

Joshlyn fixed them both a glass of ice water and then Kellen motioned them into the living room.

"Have a seat."

Joshlyn settled comfortably into the plush sofa and sipped her water.

"Would you mind if I took a quick shower and got out of these sweaty clothes?" Kellen asked, plucking at her T-shirt.

"No, of course not, but please leave the door cracked a little so I can hear you should you need something, okay?"

"Okay. I'll only be a moment. Please help yourself. There are plenty of things to snack on in the kitchen if you'd like."

Joshlyn clasped her hand and squeezed gently. "I'll be fine, Kellen. Go ahead."

Kellen looked like she was going to say something else before nodding slightly and heading off down the hall. Joshlyn watched her retreat and then sat back to relax. Being around Kellen and getting to know her was easier than Joshlyn thought it would be, although she had not anticipated being alone with her in her home. Hearing the shower start, Joshlyn stood up to look around.

The living room was very cozy. The walls were a light vanilla color and had many seascape prints adorning them. Joshlyn glanced at all the walls and noticed there were no personal pictures hanging anywhere. *How odd.* The solid oak entertainment center housed a large flat screen television and a stereo system. To the right of the entertainment center was another hallway opposite the one that Kellen had gone down. She didn't want to be too nosey so she didn't go down that hall. She peered back down the hall Kellen went. There were three doors visible from where she stood. Joshlyn studied the CDs that were stacked on the shelf closest to her. Lying partially under one of them was a picture Joshlyn had almost missed. She reached over and tugged the picture free, bringing it closer to study. The picture appeared to have been taken in a heavily treed area with lots of rocks for climbing. Next to one of the large boulders, Kellen was standing beside another woman with her arm around the woman's shoulders. They were both smiling.

"What are you doing?"

Chapter Four

Kellen stood under the hot water, letting it pelt against her, hoping the steady rhythm would loosen her already tensing neck muscles. She washed her hair, lathering it gently around the large goose egg rising above her right ear. She hissed when coming across a rather sensitive spot.

"Damn, Emerson, you clocked me a good one."

Kellen knew it was an accident, but that didn't make it hurt any less. Feeling the nausea start to surge up again, she finished rinsing, turned the water off, and pushed the shower curtain open. When she reached for the towel, she took a quick glance in the mirror. Her face was washed out and there were dark smudges starting to form under her eyes, attesting to the growing need to either vomit or fall into a deep slumber until her headache subsided.

"I look like hell. Probably going to send Joshlyn running," Kellen mumbled.

Kellen dried off and slipped into a comfortable pair of natural colored cotton lounge pants and matching button down shirt. She hung her towel and ran her fingers lightly through her hair. Taking a deep breath, she opened the door and headed back down the hall to Joshlyn.

She pulled up short of the living room when she saw Joshlyn reach for something on the entertainment center. Kellen watched the emotions play over

Joshlyn's features as she studied the picture. Her headache momentarily forgotten, Kellen's heart beat a little faster when she remembered what picture it was.

"What are you doing?" Kellen asked harshly as she stepped further into the living room.

Joshlyn jerked her head around, dropping the picture in the process.

"Uh…" Joshlyn trailed off. *Shit!* "I was just, um…" Joshlyn bent to retrieve the picture as Kellen stepped around the couch and in front of her.

Joshlyn handed the picture to her. "I'm sorry. I didn't mean to be nosey."

Kellen took the picture and placed it back on the shelf without even a cursory glance at it. The motion was not lost on Joshlyn.

The momentary silence was almost deafening. Joshlyn's racing pulse finally started to slow. She hadn't meant to upset Kellen, but it was very apparent that was exactly what she had done. She took a moment to observe this woman who puzzled her at every turn. Manicured toes peeked out from under comfortable looking pants that were tied loosely at the waist. A portion of tanned stomach peeked out from the gap left by the minimally buttoned shirt. By the time Joshlyn made it to the pale features of her face, it seemed as though Kellen had visibly relaxed.

"Listen, are you…"

"Would you like…" Joshlyn said in unison with Kellen.

Joshlyn gave a nervous laugh. "Go ahead."

Kellen smiled and tilted her head. "I was just going to ask if you were hungry. I really didn't get a chance to eat before the accident. We could order something in if you'd like."

"Mmm." Joshlyn was hedging when her stomach grumbled loud enough to be heard. Laughing, she said, "I could eat."

"All right then, follow me." Kellen headed to the kitchen and opened a drawer. "Here are a bunch of menus. Pick anything that sounds good to you because I like them all."

Joshlyn perused the menus and grabbed one that delivered. "How does this one sound?" she asked, handing the menu to Kellen.

"They have some great food. Sounds good."

Kellen called in their order and they headed back to the living room to wait. Kellen knew her behavior earlier was inappropriate, but she really didn't want to rehash anything about that picture. She felt like shit for jumping all over Joshlyn about it. *Damn it. Bite the bullet, Reynolds.*

"I want to apologize for yelling at you earlier," Kellen started.

"No, I'm sorry for messing with something that wasn't mine."

"Joshlyn, you didn't do anything wrong. I told you to make yourself at home. That picture…" Kellen stopped long enough to look down into her hands that were resting on her lap. She fidgeted for a moment and felt a warm hand on her arm. Looking back up into Joshlyn's eyes, she saw something akin to understanding and continued. "That picture brings back some memories that aren't so happy."

"It's okay. Really."

"All right. Thanks."

"So, tell me how you got into race car driving," Joshlyn asked, changing the subject.

"You know, I've been driving for as long as I

can remember. When I was younger, I always used to sit on my granddad's lap. He lived on this piece of land in a small town. He farmed for a living so there were always tractors and trucks that needed a driver." Kellen smiled as the memories filled her mind. That time in her life was probably the happiest she had ever been.

"Naturally you just took over when he needed it, huh?" Joshlyn teased.

Kellen grinned. "Something like that, yeah. That farm was hard work, but I never minded it. Granddaddy never seemed to mind showing me things either, even when it took away from getting the work done."

"He sounds like a really neat guy."

"He was and I needed that positive role model since my own father was never anywhere to be found."

Joshlyn detected a touch of bitterness in that statement and waited to see if Kellen would elaborate.

"My father was…is a horrible alcoholic. He never really acted like I was an important person in his life. You know, you try really hard to please the people who are supposed to mean something to you and eventually you give up when it goes unnoticed."

For so long Kellen had buried these feelings of animosity. It was strange to feel them bubble to the surface so easily. It shouldn't matter. *That's what you keep telling yourself. It shouldn't, but it does.*

Kellen shook her head, trying to rid herself of unwanted memories and feelings. "Anyhow, that spurred me on to bigger and better things. I was obsessed with reading as a child and once I started helping on the farm, I couldn't get my hands on enough books about women race car drivers. Women like Janet Guthrie and Lyn St. James really pioneered the way for women in the world of racing."

"Were they the first women to race?"

"Actually, the first woman driver in NASCAR history was Sara Christian."

"How long ago was that?" Joshlyn asked.

"That was in 1949. She actually didn't get to finish the race because another driver's car had engine trouble so he took over her car, but that was just the start of it. Janet Guthrie was the first woman to compete in the Indy 500."

Kellen really enjoyed discussing all facts of racing, but the women really garnered her attention. "Am I boring you yet?"

Joshlyn tipped her head slightly and smiled. "Actually just the opposite. I don't really know much about it, so this is refreshing."

"Well then, I will give you one more little fun bit of info. There was also a transgendered driver in the early '90's but she did go on to get the sex reassignment surgery by the mid '90's."

"Really?"

"Yep…fascinating, huh?"

"Definitely. So, all of this made you want to drive?"

"Just before my granddaddy died, he introduced me to his really good friend, Mason. Mason owned an auto shop and had been diligently working on this car that he wanted to get into the races. I raced with him for a while until his health failed. When he passed away his brother, Bob, approached me about driving and from there I was completely hooked. One thing led to another and here I am today."

"And that's the same company that you drive for now?"

"Yes and no. That little shop ended up getting sold after Mason passed away. This group was a part of the garage but went off on its own when the garage sold. I got involved with them about four years ago so Bob is my crew chief now."

Joshlyn nodded in understanding. "How was your relationship with your mom?"

"Apparently she died when I was six. I don't remember to be honest." Kellen cleared her throat before continuing. "I get pieces here and there that I think are memories, but who do I have that I can ask about them?"

"I'm sorry, Kellen." Joshlyn placed her hand over Kellen's and gave it gentle squeeze.

Kellen smiled. "Thanks. Are you close to your parents?"

"My father passed away and my mother, um, at one time I used to be, but now..." Joshlyn ducked her head and finished the sentence in a voice that was barely audible. "...no, not at all."

Kellen sat quietly, giving Joshlyn a moment to collect herself. As soon as she asked the question, she wished she could have taken it back. She couldn't really explain the change in Joshlyn. It was as if a wall emerged and put her on guard. The cold intonation of her voice alone made the topic unapproachable.

Kellen chewed her lower lip, trying desperately to find a way to divert the conversation. She was startled when Joshlyn spoke up and changed the subject.

"So anyhow, is driving how you occupy most of your time?"

Kellen gave a relieved chuckle. "Not really. I guess it's pretty even between the racetrack and the business."

"Wow, I'm impressed. Your driving and the business are at two different ends of the spectrum. If I'm being honest, I would say that I never would have guessed you ran that type of business."

Kellen raised both eyebrows at Joshlyn, but said nothing.

Joshlyn blushed, realizing what she had said and jumped in to do some fast backtracking. "What I meant is that just from what I know of you at the racetrack I wouldn't have guessed you would be so detail oriented—" Joshlyn stopped abruptly. "I need to stop while I'm ahead, don't I?"

Kellen laughed aloud. "You're fine. I understand what you're trying to say. It does seem kind of odd doesn't it? I guess sometimes I just need the adrenaline rush that driving gives me. There's nothing that will get the blood pumping quicker than going that fast down a stretch of open road." Kellen's thoughts went into overdrive after that comment. *There is one other thing that I know will get the blood pumping that fast, but there is no way I am going down that road right now!*

The ringing of the doorbell stopped them from pursuing the conversation further. Joshlyn got up before Kellen could and headed to the door.

"I'll get it. You just relax." Joshlyn felt warm under the collar after Kellen's last statement. She pulled her shirt slightly away from her body, trying to cool down before opening the door. *Damn, injured or not, she is sexy as hell!*

❧❧❧❧

After eating dinner and cleaning up, Joshlyn

and Kellen sat on the couch making small talk. Kellen was having a hard time keeping up with the conversation due to the dull headache that now had morphed into a full-blown attack. Reaching up to rub her forehead lightly, Kellen fought the urge to bolt for the bathroom. *Please don't let me throw up in front of her!* She closed her eyes and concentrated on taking small shallow breaths.

"Hey, are you okay?" Joshlyn gently rubbed Kellen's knee in concern. Kellen's normally tan face was pasty white.

As much as she hated to admit it, Kellen knew she couldn't hide it any longer. "This headache is making me feel a little sick to my stomach."

Joshlyn thought for a moment before responding. "Why don't I grab you some ibuprofen and then you can lie down for a little while and see if it goes away?"

"I really don't want to leave you out here all by yourself. How rude of me is that?"

"Kellen, you're hurt. I don't think that's being rude at all." Joshlyn paused before continuing. "Tell you what. Why don't you lay here on the couch and I'll sit in the chair. We can watch some TV and if you happen to fall asleep then all the better."

Kellen wavered only momentarily before agreeing. "Okay." Kellen glanced at the clock.

"If you get bored please wake me up…*if* I fall asleep."

Joshlyn smiled. "All right, sounds good." Joshlyn was not concerned about Kellen falling asleep since Emerson had checked her out and wasn't too worried.

Joshlyn stood up and asked, "Where do you keep the ibuprofen?"

"It should be on the counter next to the bathroom

sink."

Joshlyn retrieved the ibuprofen and waited while Kellen took them. She set Kellen's glass back on the end table and moved to the side to help her swing her feet up and lay down.

Joshlyn bent down to help Kellen shift the throw pillow a little further under her head. She watched as Kellen's eyes closed before laying a hand on her upper arm and caressing gently. "Are you warm enough or would you like this throw blanket over you?" Joshlyn asked, gesturing towards the blanket on the back of the couch.

"No, I'm okay, but thank you."

Joshlyn could tell by the vague response that Kellen was not feeling well. She barely raised her head and didn't open her eyes when Joshlyn spoke to her. Joshlyn watched her for a moment longer before taking her seat and turning the TV on.

❧ ❧ ❧ ❧

Not even a half hour had gone by when Joshlyn heard Kellen moaning. There was no question in Joshlyn's mind that Kellen would fall asleep, especially when she looked half-asleep before her head hit the pillow. Getting quietly to her feet, Joshlyn moved closer to the couch. She leaned down to see if she could hear what Kellen was moaning about, but the only word she was able to understand was 'no.'

"Kellen?" Joshlyn tried calling her name before touching her, but there was no response. "Kellen?"

Again getting no reaction, Joshlyn reached lightly for Kellen's shoulder. She immediately became alarmed at the dampness that permeated Kellen's clothing and covered her face. Joshlyn gently brushed the hair away from Kellen's face and cupped a palm against her cheek. *She doesn't feel like she's running a fever. Must be one hell of a dream.*

"Kellen? C'mon, wake up for me."

Joshlyn watched as confused blue eyes opened briefly before closing again. Taking a deep breath, Joshlyn decided to throw caution to the wind. She kicked her shoes off and then lifted Kellen's head enough to slip underneath her. Kellen instantly turned towards her and snuggled down. Joshlyn grabbed the throw blanket off the back of the couch and spread it over them the best she could.

Joshlyn ran her fingers through Kellen's hair, avoiding the lump she knew had to be very sensitive. She gazed down into Kellen's face and saw the tense muscles begin to relax. She caressed Kellen's head a couple more times before moving her hand down to run a finger gently across a dark eyebrow. Following the eyebrow, she traced a line down the side of her face and rested her fingertips against Kellen's neck. She moved her fingers to the back of Kellen's neck and started a gentle massage.

Kellen moaned, mumbled a few incoherent words, and nuzzled closer to Joshlyn's body.

Joshlyn bent down and asked, "What did you say, Kellen?"

Kellen kept her eyes closed, but rolled her head back a little and mumbled again. "I didn't mean for you to die."

Chapter Five

Kellen snuggled deeper into the softness her cheek was resting against. She sighed in contentment, keeping her eyes closed. The atmosphere around her was very quiet, except for the precise tick of the clock on the wall. She thought of the events that had taken place in the last twenty-four hours and smiled. Even though it took a knock in the head to get some alone time with Joshlyn, it was more than worth it. As she recalled their evening and how it ended, she opened her eyes and sighed in disappointment when she encountered the fabric on the back of the couch.

"Son of a bitch," she whispered, blinking her eyes into focus.

Kellen rolled to her back and then slowly sat up. The headache and nausea seemed to be gone. She ran her fingers through her tousled hair, feeling gingerly for the lump. While doing so, she looked about the living room. There was no Joshlyn and no note.

She got to her feet and trudged to the bathroom. Just as she reached for the handle, the door opened. Kellen jumped back, heart beating wildly, and found herself face to face with Joshlyn.

Joshlyn gave a startled yelp and placed a hand on her chest. "God, Kellen, I am so sorry. I didn't expect you to be awake yet."

"It's okay," Kellen said with a chuckle. "I thought you had already left."

"No, I was going to, but you were having kind of a rough night. I called Ami and told her I was going to stay." Joshlyn hesitated before continuing. "Is that okay?"

Kellen heard what Joshlyn said, but wasn't actually listening. Joshlyn's freshly scrubbed face and unruly hair looked adorable. Kellen smiled at her appearance.

"Kellen?"

Kellen refocused and replied, "I'm sorry, what did you say?"

Joshlyn gave Kellen a confused look. "I asked if it was okay that I stayed."

"Oh, yes, that's fine, no problem."

"Okay…Uh, are you feeling all right this morning?"

Kellen could not remember a time when she stood in her hall, outside the bathroom no less, and made small talk with anyone, much less someone she really wanted to get to know better. It all seemed somewhat surreal.

"Yeah, I'm feeling pretty good. The nausea is gone and the headache is hardly noticeable."

Joshlyn stepped forward. "How about that bump?"

As Joshlyn moved closer, Kellen sucked in a breath. She stared at Joshlyn's lips as she threaded her fingers through Kellen's hair to locate the bump. She knew that if she kept focusing on Joshlyn's mouth she'd find herself in trouble. Kellen closed her eyes and relaxed under Joshlyn's touch.

"You can barely feel it now."

"Hmm," Kellen responded. Her scalp literally tingled where Joshlyn's fingers roamed.

Joshlyn slowly pulled her hand from Kellen's hair and let her palm open against Kellen's cheek. "Did I hurt you?"

"No," Kellen whispered, keeping her eyes closed.

Joshlyn watched as Kellen's lips parted and the tip of her tongue came out to moisten them. She was torn between stepping back or doing what she so badly wanted to do. And make no mistake, she wanted this, she wanted this more than anything. She leaned closer until she could feel Kellen's warm breath against her face.

"Kellen, look at me."

Kellen opened her eyes and met Joshlyn's gaze. *Oh my God! I am definitely in trouble.*

"Please," Kellen said in a husky rasp.

Joshlyn's heart pounded inside her chest, her body strumming with anticipation. The war going on between her head and heart kept Joshlyn's feet rooted.

Kellen must have sensed her hesitation because she glanced away briefly, cleared her throat, and pinned her with pleading eyes. "Please kiss me, Joshlyn."

Joshlyn closed the distance and felt Kellen's warm lips against hers. The torrent heat of the kiss built until it exploded in raw passion. Joshlyn let the kiss continue for a few more moments before pulling back and looking directly into Kellen's face. She had never wanted someone as badly as she wanted Kellen right now. The heat in her belly spread throughout her body, her fingers begging to be all over Kellen. To touch and taste every inch of her, coaxing a response little by little until the fervor was too much and sent them both over the edge. *This is insane...she is making me insane!*

Kellen tried desperately to control her breathing

and rapid pulse, but was failing miserably. *Fuck it!*

Kellen reached for her at the same time Joshlyn stepped forward. Kellen wrapped her arms around Joshlyn and pulled her flush against her chest. Breast to breast, Kellen lowered her lips to Joshlyn's this time and let the fire consume them.

Joshlyn's lips parted at the first touch of Kellen's tongue. She slid her hands into the back of Kellen's hair and pulled her head impossibly closer.

Kellen backed Joshlyn into the wall behind them and insinuated a thigh between her legs. Things were spiraling out of control fast and Kellen knew if they didn't stop soon she'd probably do something that neither of them was ready for.

Kellen slowly ended the kiss and pulled her head back. The desire-filled look in Joshlyn's eyes just about ended her act of chivalry. She placed one last simple kiss on Joshlyn's swollen lips and leaned back.

Joshlyn remained against the wall, but grabbed one of Kellen's hands so she couldn't go too far.

"Wow, that was…" Joshlyn couldn't even begin to put words to what she was feeling. Well, aside from being extremely turned on.

Kellen grinned. "Yeah, my thoughts exactly."

Joshlyn's smile grew until they were both chuckling.

Kellen tugged playfully at Joshlyn's hand and said, "Let's take our showers and then we can figure something out for breakfast."

At Joshlyn's raised eyebrows and cocky grin, Kellen rolled her eyes. "Separate showers or else we'll both be in trouble," Kellen warned.

"Chicken."

"Absolutely!" Kellen laughed. "I've got some

clothes you can wear. C'mon."

Kellen took two steps and stopped. "On the other hand, maybe you should wait here."

Joshlyn grinned and gave her a light push towards the bedroom. "Your virtue is safe with me."

⚜ ⚜ ⚜ ⚜

Joshlyn sat with one leg tucked under her while she watched Kellen load their breakfast plates into the dishwasher. After arguing over who was going to do the dishes, Joshlyn finally relented. She took a sip of coffee and set it down. Propping her chin in her hand, she admired the grace with which Kellen moved about the kitchen. She made even the most mundane tasks look sexy. Joshlyn grinned at the view of Kellen's backside as she bent over to put one last dish in before closing the dishwasher. A groan worked its way up Joshlyn's throat only to be tampered down at the last minute. The ache that had been awakened in Joshlyn's libido was making her squirm.

Kellen dried her hands and dropped the towel on the counter. She turned towards Joshlyn and caught the smile that she was sure she wasn't supposed to see, considering Joshlyn's eyes were not on her face, but at waist level. Kellen cleared her throat and smirked as Joshlyn's eyes flew to her own.

"So," Kellen said, walking over and taking a seat at the table. "You mentioned that I had a rough night last night. What exactly did you mean?"

Joshlyn took a moment while her furious blush was fading to contemplate whether she should tell Kellen what was said or to let it go. Part of her was curious to know what the statement meant, but the other part was afraid to know the exact details. Curiosity won.

"You were moaning and mumbling in your sleep. At first I was concerned because I thought maybe the head injury was causing it." Joshlyn paused to take another sip of coffee. With her hands wrapped around the mug, she continued. "You didn't seem to be running a fever so my next thought was that you were having a dream. I tried to wake you up, but was not successful. Finally, I slipped my shoes off and slid underneath you to try and comfort you in hopes that you would settle down."

Joshlyn set the cup down and looked directly into Kellen's eyes. "You did calm down and sleep peacefully from then on. However, before you did there was something you said that has me a little curious."

Kellen tried to remember what she could have possibly said, but was drawing a complete blank. "What? What did I say?"

"You said, 'I didn't mean for you to die.'"

Kellen visibly blanched at the statement, but said nothing. She glanced away and then down into her own cup. *Damn! I can't believe how fast this is coming up.*

Joshlyn laid a hand over Kellen's and spoke softly. "Kellen, you don't have to talk about it if you don't want to."

Kellen thought about avoiding the issue all together, but if there was to be anything between them, she wanted to start out with her cards on the table. She took a deep breath and glanced at Joshlyn. Her resolve broke at the understanding she could see in Joshlyn's eyes.

"No, I want you to know. There may be times when I have to stop, though."

"That's up to you, Kellen, but just know that you can stop anytime you want, and I promise I won't be upset."

Kellen nodded. "I've told you a little about my father, and I'm sure that by now you have a pretty good idea how angry the whole situation made me while growing up."

"I'd say you had just cause for being angry, though," Joshlyn replied.

"Yes, and that anger made me very unapproachable. I didn't have many friends through high school. It wasn't until I started college that I actually had people I considered to be true friends. There were four of us to a room and the other three decided they weren't going to put up with my brooding and sour attitude all the time." Kellen smiled, remembering some of the antics the girls got away with.

"One of the girls eventually became my best friend. We did everything together. She's the woman in that picture you saw last night."

"What is her name?" Joshlyn asked quietly.

"Kerri," Kellen said with a wistful smile. "Kerri, Molly, Erin, and I spent most of our weekends together, but Kerri and I spent almost all our free time together; weekdays, weekends, holidays, it just didn't matter. They were determined that I was not going to ruin their free time and even more determined that I wasn't going to spend it alone. Do you have any idea how hard it was to fight three of them?"

Joshlyn laughed, but didn't say anything. She waited patiently until Kellen was ready to continue.

"The thing that bonded Kerri and I was that we were both into some of the more extreme or daring things. We bungee jumped several times, which was big for me because I'm somewhat afraid of heights. Whitewater rafting was always fun, but our biggest pleasure was rock climbing. I know you are wondering why rock climbing when I'm afraid of heights, but that was the beauty of it. Kerri always made me feel secure and for the most part, I am over that fear. We made this pact that every year we'd spend a week together and rock climb somewhere."

"Were you and Kerri ever intimately involved?"

Kellen smiled at Joshlyn's question. She had heard it more times than she could count. "No, she was as straight as they come, but I did love her very much. She and the other girls became my family."

Kellen got up to refill her coffee cup and sat back down. She stirred some sugar into her cup and reached for the creamer. Her thumb flicked at the label on the container briefly before she poured some in.

"Four years ago, we went rock climbing in Oregon. Kerri didn't really want to go because she had some things at work that she needed to get done. I pestered her until she finally agreed. On the drive there we did a lot of talking because I knew Kerri was upset that I had basically forced her into going." Kellen stopped talking and turned in her chair so she was facing Joshlyn.

"She needed a break in the worst way, Joshlyn. She had lost weight, wasn't sleeping, and I was really worried. I thought if I could get her away that maybe she'd feel better. About ten hours into the trip, she finally forgave me and agreed that a break was what she needed. We took our time and made several stops along the way. We had taken almost two weeks off for this trip because we knew the driving time would eat up a lot of hours."

Kellen propped her arm over the back of the chair and rested her chin on her arm. She reflected back on the drive and chuckled at some of the silly things they came across at the different gas stations. "Have you ever noticed all the raunchy stuff that gas stations along the main interstates sell?"

Joshlyn laughed with her and chimed right in. "Yeah, my favorite are the little machines that have the uh, little surprises for only seventy-five cents."

"Does anyone ever buy that stuff?" Kellen asked.

"Oh, c'mon, you mean to tell me you never bought any just to see what it was?"

"No way," Kellen said, shaking her head. "I'd have spent my money on anything else rather than waste it on that."

Joshlyn agreed and then settled down so Kellen could continue.

"Anyhow, the trip was a blast. There are some beautiful sights in those rocks. We took lots of pictures. That picture you saw was taken on our last day there." Kellen stopped, feeling her heart beating a little faster she took some slow breaths.

Joshlyn knew the hard part for Kellen was coming. The fine layer of perspiration on her face and her fidgeting hands attested to the fact that this was going to be difficult for her.

"We had made it to the top of this ridge and stopped for a short break. Another couple was preparing to head down. They stopped long enough to snap a picture for us and then proceeded on their way. Neither one of us spoke for a while, knowing that this was our last climb of the trip."

Kellen turned back around in her chair and placed both arms on the table. She stared at the liquid in her cup as though it weren't there. Images flooded her memory from that day.

"The climb back down seemed to take a lot longer, but we both were always very meticulous about taking our time and being safe. Kerri had started down first and was maybe six feet below me most of the time. About a third of the way down I heard something snap. I didn't have a chance to even react."

Joshlyn kept a close eye on Kellen, knowing full well that her agitation was increasing. The pulse in the side of her neck was getting faster and faster.

"I looked down and couldn't see Kerri anywhere. I screamed her name, but she never said a word. I...I..." Kellen jerked in reaction, as if reliving the whole thing again. "The next thing I heard was a thud and then everything was silent."

Joshlyn jumped up, grabbing a towel to wipe up the coffee Kellen had spilled when her hands jerked. Kellen was unaware that she had spilled it until Joshlyn started cleaning it up. Setting the towel down, Joshlyn pulled her chair closer to Kellen's.

"I'm here, sweetie."

Kellen turned towards Joshlyn and continued. "She never had a chance. She landed in a crevasse and was wedged pretty tight. When they finally got her out, she was barely alive. There was a significant head injury and several other broken bones. I'm pretty sure they knew she wasn't going to make it before they ever airlifted her off the ground."

Pools of moisture gathered in Kellen's eyes until finally twin trails of tears ran down her face. The renewed pain in her chest from the heartache of that day made breathing difficult. She tried hard to contain the sob lurking at the surface, but it was too much. She made one last attempt before giving in to the sorrow.

Joshlyn stood up and pulled Kellen against her. She held her close, whispering soothing words and caressing her hair. "I'm so, so sorry, Kellen."

Chapter Six

Joshlyn rubbed Kellen's back a couple more times before settling her hand lightly on her shoulder. She tilted her head as she glanced down, trying to catch Kellen's attention. Kellen leaned back and scrubbed at her eyes with her fingertips. She dropped her hands to her lap and looked up into Joshlyn's sympathetic eyes.

"That was the reason I said that to you last night. I always felt guilty because Kerri didn't even want to go on that trip. I felt like it was my fault."

"Kellen, surely you know that it wasn't your fault. You're not responsible for the equipment failure."

Kellen nodded. "I know that now, but…" Kellen looked away briefly before continuing. "At the time I felt I was responsible and the guilt consumed me. After the funeral, I secluded myself. I wouldn't answer the phone, didn't look at my mail…nothing. I wasn't eating, not getting enough sleep."

Joshlyn placed a hand over Kellen's. "What changed all that?"

Kellen smiled and then chuckled. "More like who. Erin and Molly showed up after six months of putting up with my crap. They took charge. They made me eat and then take a shower while they cleaned the house. Afterwards they made me sit down and tell them what was going on."

"They sound like really good friends."

"They are. When I finished telling them how I felt, Erin got up and placed a call. Next thing I know she's handing me a piece of paper with a date and time on it. She had set up an appointment for me with a therapist. Linda, the therapist, was a friend of Erin's and she trusted her implicitly to help me through my grief. I went to the appointment and made consecutive appointments for nine months."

Kellen took a sip of her now tepid coffee and set it back on the table. "Those appointments and the steady work on that deck are what kept me sane. I eventually accepted that the accident wasn't my fault, but every now and then it really hits me."

"I can understand that. Kerri was a big part of your life. You can move about each day like it doesn't matter, but fact is that sometimes it's good to cry about the things you miss." Joshlyn stood, grabbed her cup, and walked over to the counter. "It doesn't mean that you are harboring any feelings of guilt or that you're not over it. It simply means that they existed and they mattered."

Kellen turned in her chair and stared at Joshlyn's back. *I wonder if she's referring to me or someone else?*

Joshlyn dumped the remnants of her coffee down the drain and placed her cup in the dishwasher. She took a deep breath and turned back towards Kellen.

"Do you know what I mean?"

Kellen smiled and nodded. "I do. It makes a lot of sense."

The silence stretched between them as they stared into each other's eyes. Kellen stood up and took a step forward. Joshlyn closed the distance between them and stopped in front of Kellen. Kellen opened her arms and Joshlyn stepped into them, wrapping her arms around Kellen's waist.

"Thank you for yesterday and for being here last night with me. I really appreciate it," Kellen said in almost a whisper.

"You're welcome, Kellen."

Kellen rested her lips against the top of Joshlyn's head and gave her a light kiss. Squeezing her gently, Kellen stepped back from the warm embrace.

"I guess I better get you home, huh?"

Joshlyn smiled. "I guess so."

❧❧❧❧

Kellen followed the directions Joshlyn gave her as they chatted about nothing in particular on the drive to her house.

"So when is the next race?" Joshlyn asked.

"Next Saturday. Would you like to come?"

Joshlyn smiled. "I'd love to."

Kellen glanced briefly her direction before returning her eyes to the road. "Great. Hey, would you like to stand down in the pit area during the race?"

"Wow, really? I mean, I could do that?" Joshlyn was getting excited. To watch the race was one thing, but to be down in the actual pit area during the race would be fantastic.

Kellen shrugged. "Sure. Oh, and if Ami wants to come, too, that would be all right."

"I'll ask her if she wants to go, but either way I'll be there." Joshlyn reached across the console, laced her fingers through Kellen's, and squeezed.

Kellen returned the gesture and smiled. She pulled into Joshlyn's driveway, but was reluctant to release her hand. She was enjoying the contact between the two of them.

Joshlyn slowly released Kellen's hand so she could put the vehicle in park. She watched as Kellen turned the key and cut the engine. Turning in her seat, she smiled at Kellen.

"Would you mind if I brought my cameras with me?"

"No, not at all." Kellen grinned at Joshlyn's excitement.

"Will you call me tonight? I mean, I want to know that you're doing okay and not having any problems from the accident."

"I can do that, but I'm sure I'll be just fine."

"I'm sure you will, but I'd just feel better knowing."

Kellen grabbed a pen and piece of paper and jotted down her number. "I'll show you mine if you show me yours," she said teasingly, handing the paper in Joshlyn's direction.

Joshlyn grinned, tore the paper in half, and wrote her number down. She placed a hand on the console and leaned closer to Kellen. Closing the last bit of space between them, Joshlyn kissed Kellen gently on the lips. "Thank you," she whispered.

Kellen smiled and placed a return kiss on Joshlyn's lips. "You're welcome. I'll call you tonight."

⁂

After returning home, Kellen turned on the stereo and picked up the photo of her and Kerri. It really was a good picture with both of them smiling and looking happy. She propped the picture up next to a couple of CDs and turned to look about the living room. The house seemed quiet and empty without Joshlyn being there. *She was only here one time!*

Kellen plopped down on the couch and patted it, waiting for Chigger to join her. She scratched him lightly behind the ears. "That's not a bad thing, now is it, Chigger?" The dog ignored her, but shifted so she was now scratching his belly. "I mean, look at her. She's gorgeous and those lips. My God, they are so sweet. Just her fingers in my hair drives me crazy."

Kellen groaned and dropped her head to the back of the couch. Staring at the ceiling, she rolled her head from side to side. "I am so gone, buddy."

It wasn't that Kellen was lacking for dates, because she had dated often up until recently. The fact remained that none of them had ever captured her interest, and made her want to pursue those feelings, like Joshlyn had. She hoped that this was the start of something really good.

Kellen reached over and grabbed the phone off the coffee table. She punched in a number and waited for it to be answered.

"Hello?"

"Hey, Erin. What are you up to today?"

"Kellen Anne Reynolds. Why has it taken you so long to call me?"

Kellen laughed. "I've been busy. The business has been keeping me really busy lately."

"Ahuh. Just don't forget family, you hear?" Erin admonished.

"I hear you, geesh," Kellen grumbled good-naturedly. "Listen, do you want to get together one night this week for dinner?"

"I'll go one even better. How about you come over, I'll cook, and we can watch a movie or just sit and chat. How does that sound?"

"Perfect."

They chatted a little longer, setting a date and time for dinner, and then said their goodbyes.

Kellen set the phone down and roused Chigger. "C'mon boy, let's go for a walk." Chigger immediately perked up at the word 'walk' and jumped down off the couch. She grabbed his leash, clicked it on, and stepped out the door.

∿∿∿

Joshlyn closed the door and leaned heavily against it. The time spent with Kellen was the most she had enjoyed spending with anyone lately, even under the circumstances. She pulled the collar of her shirt up and sniffed appreciatively at it. The scent was all Kellen; her laundry soap, softener, and shower gel all wrapped in one delectable aroma.

She was pulled from her musings by the ringing telephone.

"Hello?"

"Joshlyn? I was wondering when you were going to call me. I've called a couple times this morning already."

"Sorry, Ami. I just got home."

"Ah, I see. I just wanted to make sure that everything was okay. Is Kellen feeling all right?"

Joshlyn sat down in the chair and toed her sneakers off. "Yep, she's doing just fine. She didn't seem to have any after effects this morning. The lump was almost gone as well."

"That's good. Emerson felt so bad. He's as competitive as the next person, but not at the expense of somebody getting hurt."

"Well, tell him to relax because Kellen doesn't hold it against him. She knows it was an accident."

Ami was silent for a moment, not sure if she should ask her next question, but proceeded anyhow. "So, how did things go with her?"

"They were just fine. No problems."

"Joshlyn, quit being so nonchalant with me. You know what I'm asking."

Joshlyn smiled. "Not very subtle there."

"Screw that, now give!"

Joshlyn laughed. "That woman intrigues the hell out of me. I don't know what it is about her, but I like her, Ami. I like her a lot."

"So? What does this mean?"

"You are so damned nosey—" Joshlyn stopped as Ami's laughter interrupted. She waited until Ami settled down before continuing. "It means that I'm going to let things happen and take it from there. I want to get to know her better."

"That is a fantastic idea. From what Emerson has said, she's a real sweetheart and you could do much worse."

"I'm glad you approve," Joshlyn replied, sarcastically.

"Oh, you know I've been trying to fix you up forever. I'm just happy that someone has garnered your attention enough for you to follow through and see what'll happen."

"Yeah, yeah. She invited me to the races next weekend and I get to go down to the pit and watch it from there. Do you want to come along?"

"That sounds exciting. Normally I'd jump at the chance, but Jaxon is in town next weekend so I doubt

I'll be out doing much at all."

Joshlyn blushed at the underlying message Ami was sharing with her. Jaxon was a wonderful man and generous to a fault. She couldn't blame Ami for wanting to spend the weekend alone at home.

"Some other time then. I'm going to take my cameras so hopefully I'll get some good pictures."

"Great. I can't wait to see them. I'm glad Kellen's okay. I better run for now, but I'll talk to you later, sweetie."

"Have a great morning, Ami."

Joshlyn hung up and tapped the phone lightly against her chin. She was really looking forward to next weekend and hoped the week itself would fly by. The past three years were difficult because Joshlyn used to be an outgoing, fun-loving person. Always had something going on or somewhere to be and she never really minded. It wasn't until that was all taken away that a person realizes how much they truly missed. She wanted this chance with Kellen and if that meant letting more of her guard down then that's what she would have to do.

"Who could walk away from those tantalizing kisses?" Joshlyn whispered.

Chapter Seven

Joshlyn rolled over and slapped the alarm off. She pushed the hair out of her face and stretched.

Joshlyn moaned as she finished her stretch. "Mmmm, it's race day." She grinned. "Race day…" she said again, letting the words roll off her tongue. *Who would have thought I'd be this excited for a race? It's not exactly the race that has me excited, though that is a definite bonus!*

Kellen had called almost every night. At first, there was always a reason, but the last few nights she really had no excuse. Conversation was easy flowing and Joshlyn found herself not wanting it to end.

Joshlyn smiled, thinking back on one particular conversation. She barely made it to the phone before it quit ringing.

"Hello?" *Joshlyn said, trying to catch her breath.*

"Hey there. Did I catch you at a bad time?" Kellen asked.

"No, no, not at all. I just got home and was rushing to get the phone before you hung up."

"Ah, well, I'm glad you did," Kellen responded, smiling to herself.

"Me, too."

There was a comfortable, yet intimate silence before Joshlyn spoke again.

"So, Saturday is coming up here pretty quick. Are

you still sure about me coming to the race and being down in the pit?"

"Of course I'm sure. I wouldn't have asked if I didn't mean it. I think it will be a lot of fun."

Joshlyn chuckled. "For me or for you?"

Kellen grinned and replied, "For both, naturally."

"Naturally," Joshlyn agreed.

"Besides, what better incentive than to have you waiting for me after the race? Hmm?"

"You know, I never thought of it that way."

"See?" Kellen laughed. "Seriously though, I love racing and to share that with someone I..." Kellen hesitated and changed her line of thought. "To share that with you makes me very happy."

Joshlyn didn't comment on Kellen's choice of words, but instead replied quietly, "I'm really looking forward to it, Kellen."

"Me, too."

"Ok, so what about it excites you so much? I mean, you've mentioned the adrenaline rush, but what else?"

"You mean aside from my competitive nature?" Kellen laughed. "Well, it really is a lot like my software designing in many ways. It's about precision and proper decision making."

"What do you mean?"

"If I make a move at the wrong time it can have drastic effects. It's about speed and accelerating and braking at the right time. You have to take in track conditions and make adjustments. It's..." Kellen stopped, twisting her lips in thought. "I don't know, it's just...it's just...everything." Kellen cleared her throat. "Sorry about that. I could go on and on. Are you sorry for asking now?"

"Not at all. You're passionate about what you do and that's very admirable."

Joshlyn could hear the intensity in Kellen's explanation. She wished they had had the conversation in person so Joshlyn could see the passion as well.

Rolling out of bed, Joshlyn headed to the shower. She needed time to check her equipment before Kellen arrived.

❧❧❧❧

Kellen finished her breakfast and put her dishes in the dishwasher. Crouching down, she scratched Chigger under the chin.

"You ready for your chow chow now, big boy?"

Chigger's hind end and tail wiggled as much as it possibly could for his size. He was always ready to eat.

Kellen set a bowl of food down for Chigger and watched him eat. When she first got him, Chigger was so timid he wouldn't even eat in front of her. He'd grab a few bites and then go hide to eat them. She knew he had been abused, but to what extent she'd never know. Now Chigger didn't even mind making a pig out of himself in front of her and nothing could make her happier. Well, almost nothing.

"It's going to be a good day, boy. I'm taking Joshlyn to the race."

Chigger raised his head at the mention of Joshlyn's name, making Kellen laugh.

"You like her already, huh?"

She patted his rump, saying, "Yeah, me too, boy. Me, too." Standing, Kellen glanced at the clock. She had just enough time to get her gear, let Chigger out, and then head over to pick Joshlyn up.

Kellen pulled up outside Joshlyn's house just as Joshlyn was coming out the door. She hopped out of the SUV and ran around to open the door.

Flashing a smile, Kellen said, "Hi."

Joshlyn's eyes met Kellen's and she smiled in return. "Hi, yourself. I hope you haven't been waiting long."

"No, not at all," Kellen responded without breaking eye contact. "Matter of fact, I just got here so it was perfect timing."

Joshlyn shouldered her camera bag and climbed into the vehicle. She could feel the heat of Kellen's gaze on her and wanted to tell her to stop. Not because it annoyed her, but because of how that look made her body react. There was something dangerously sexy about a smoldering look, especially when that person had no idea that's how they looked. Joshlyn wondered briefly if Kellen would see the same in her own eyes. Would she know how Joshlyn felt by looking into the depth of her eyes or would she see the secrets and lies that Joshlyn constantly kept hidden? *Give it a rest, Joshlyn; we'll cross that bridge IF we get there!*

Joshlyn snapped her seat belt and fiddled with the clasp on her camera bag while Kellen hopped back into the SUV and reached for her seat belt. She stopped in mid-motion and watched Joshlyn, who was fidgeting with her camera bag as if she was nervous. Her bent head and pink cheeks made Kellen wonder what was going through her mind.

Acting on instinct alone, Kellen let go of the seat belt and leaned over the console towards Joshlyn. Slowly she brought her hand up to lay it against Joshlyn's cheek. When Joshlyn looked up at her,

Kellen bent her head close and captured Joshlyn's lips with her own.

The kiss was meant to assure. It was a kiss to say, "I'm glad you're here." The kiss gradually became more as Joshlyn's arms came up and closed around Kellen, pulling her even closer.

Joshlyn moaned as Kellen's tongue insinuated itself between her lips. She wanted this woman more than she wanted anything at this very moment. She let the kiss continue for a moment longer before pulling back.

Joshlyn kissed Kellen lightly on the lips and smiled. "If we don't get a move on, I'm afraid you might not make it to your race at all."

"We could always skip this race if you wanted," Kellen said, wiggling her eyebrows.

Joshlyn laughed. "Oh no, you promised me pictures and pits so buckle up and let's hit the road."

"Yes ma'am," Kellen said, giving a mock salute.

"Is it true that race cars don't have speedometers?" Joshlyn asked once they hit the main road.

"That is true."

"Why is that? How do you know how fast you're going?"

"Well, all tires are different which affects the speed. So instead all cars use tachometers which measure the number of revolutions or turns per minute also known as RPM's." Kellen hesitated, making sure Joshlyn was following along.

"Okay."

"The revolutions indicate how hard the engine is working. Without going into a bunch of boring details, let's just say that the higher the RPM's, the faster the speed."

"Ah, ok. And they don't have keys to start the car either?"

"Nope. There are a lot of differences between stock cars and regular cars you see on the road every day."

"Which is why the tires look different, too?"

Kellen grinned. "Exactly. The more rubber touching the track the better traction you'll have. That's why there are no treads on the tires either."

"Hence the reason races are not run if it's raining."

"Right! You catch on quick."

Joshlyn blew on her nails and rubbed them on her shirt. "I'm trying. How disappointed would you be if I told you I checked a few websites to learn a few things?"

Kellen laughed before responding. "I wouldn't be disappointed at all. We all have to learn somehow, right?"

"Yep. I have to be honest though. I probably wouldn't even bother if it wasn't for you."

"I'm flattered," Kellen said, blushing.

The remainder of the drive was made with some bantering back and forth about the track, the other drivers, and Kellen's car. Time passed quickly and before Kellen knew it, they were already pulling into the gates of the track.

"Ah, here we are." Kellen parked the SUV and they made their way through the link fence to the pit. As they grew closer, Kellen reached over and clasped Joshlyn's hand in hers.

"Don't want you to get lost."

Joshlyn gave her a funny look. "How would I get lost here? Trust me; I plan on following your every step."

"Ok, then I wouldn't want the pit lizards to hound you. How's that for honesty?"

"Pit lizards?" Joshlyn asked with a chuckle.

"That would be the groupies who hang out down here just waiting to snag a driver. You have to watch your back with them. They are a ruthless bunch of women."

"You're kidding, right?"

"Unfortunately, no. It's happened before and it'll happen again."

"Point well taken," Joshlyn said, tightening her grip on Kellen's.

They walked through the garage area and passed car after car. Kellen stopped a couple times to say hello to a couple fellow drivers before stopping next to a car that Joshlyn knew was not hers.

"This is Emerson's car. I just want to say hello before we move on down to mine, ok?"

"Sure. I'd like to see him again, too."

Kellen walked around the back of the car. "Watch your step here."

Joshlyn stepped over some power cords and followed Kellen through a flap in the tent.

"Hey there, Emerson. How's it going?"

Emerson stood up and shook Kellen's hand before giving Joshlyn a quick one-arm hug.

"Hey. It's a going. You ready for today?"

"More than ready and I even brought along Joshlyn to cheer us along. Although I think she's going to take some snapshots, too."

Joshlyn didn't return Emerson's hug, but oddly enough didn't feel too uncomfortable. Maybe it was quite possible that she finally found she didn't need to feel jumpy every time she turned around. At the mention of snapshots, she brought her attention back to the conversation.

"Do you mind if I take pictures of you, too, Emerson?"

"Shoot, I don't mind at all. You snap to your heart's desire. Maybe I could talk you out of some once you get them printed."

"Absolutely."

Emerson put a hand on Kellen's shoulder and got a grim look on his face. "Listen, K, I thought I should tell you before someone else does that this race might not be as easy and lighthearted as we had hoped it would be."

"Oh, why is that?"

"Your friend and mine decided to make an appearance today."

Kellen started pacing and shaking a hand back and forth. "No, no, no...not today. Please say not today?"

"I'm sorry, Kellen," Emerson said, nodding his head.

"Son of a fucking bitch!" Kellen hissed before sitting down and putting her head in her hands.

Chapter Eight

Listen, K, I'm sure things will be fine. We just have to keep our heads up out there and watch our backs," Emerson said. He knew Kellen wasn't going to handle the news well.

"What the hell is he doing here? I thought Billy Baker was banned from the circuit."

"I don't mean to interrupt, but who is Billy Baker?" Joshlyn asked, looking between the two.

"Billy Baker was…is a fellow circuit driver. Two years ago he caused one of the biggest fuck-ups in this track's history." Emerson paused long enough to glance quickly at Kellen. She looked as disgusted now as she did the day it happened.

"Problem is that it happened right out there on pit road. You're only supposed to be going a certain speed so accidents don't happen, but Billy came off the track and didn't slow down much."

"Much? You have got to be kidding me, Emerson!" Kellen responded haughtily. "I don't think he slowed down at all. If he had then we wouldn't have lost Peetie. Peetie never even saw him coming."

Kellen stood and paced back and forth in front of Joshlyn. Her furrowed brows and twisted lips told Joshlyn all she needed to know about how Kellen felt about Billy.

"So if that's the case then how is he here racing today?" Joshlyn asked.

Kellen threw her hands in the air. "That's what I'd like to know!"

"Billy was suspended while an investigation took place. From what I heard, they put him on two-year probation, but he sent an inquiry in asking them to take a better look at his engine. He says that the engine locked up or something like that and he wasn't able to slow down."

"Engine locked up my ass! That doesn't affect your Goddamned brakes! Emerson, you didn't see the look on his face after the accident. There was no remorse there whatsoever. He didn't give two shits that his carelessness caused the death of one mechanic and the injuries of two others!"

"I know, K, I know." Emerson stuck his hands up in surrender. "Listen, you have to put this behind you. It's gonna eat you alive if you don't."

"I'll put it behind me the day that piece of shit pays for what he did!" Kellen said as she stormed back into the tent.

❧ ❧ ❧ ❧

Kellen knew she needed to cool down and felt horrible that she'd walked away, leaving Joshlyn standing there. She didn't want Joshlyn to see this ugly side of her and was embarrassed she couldn't keep it under control.

Kellen had no more than rounded Emerson's car when she ran smack into the person she loathed more than anything right now. Billy hadn't changed at all since the last time she'd seen him. His long stringy hair still looked like you could ring a vat of grease out of it. She swore he had more teeth missing than he had in his head.

"Whoa there lil' lady. You better watch where yer goin' before someone gets hurt," Billy said, grabbing Kellen by the arms.

Kellen yanked her arms away and took a step closer. "Don't you *ever* touch me again."

"Hey, I's just walkin' here when you ran inta me."

"Stay away from me, Baker," Kellen said, her voice rising with each word.

"Whatsa matter, Kellen? Ya act like ya done lost yer best friend or somethin'," Billy said with a crooked grin.

"You lousy son of a…"

❧❧❧❧

Emerson sighed and looked at Joshlyn. "Peetie was a good friend and one of the best mechanics. He'd been working with Kellen's team from the start."

"Was Billy responsible for what happened or did his engine really lock up?"

"I honestly don't know, Joshlyn, but everything seemed fine before that. To make matters worse, it's like Billy knows how much he gets under Kellen's skin." Emerson scratched his head before continuing. "He always talks smack when he's around, but after the accident he started making comments. Comments that seemed more like threats."

"Threats?"

"Yeah. Suffice it to say that they always set Kellen off."

"That's not—" Joshlyn stopped mid-sentence when a loud commotion from inside the tent drew their attention.

Emerson ran for the tent with Joshlyn close behind.

❧ ❧ ❧ ❧

"Git her the fuck away from me!" Billy yelled from his spot on the ground.

Two other drivers were standing a couple feet away with Kellen promptly subdued between them. Billy had his hands between his legs, cradling his genitals.

"You want to start some shit? Then let's go, but you damn well better be ready to finish it. I'm done with you, Baker!" Kellen sneered.

Joshlyn walked quietly over to Kellen and took her hand.

"Hey," Joshlyn said, trying to get Kellen's attention. "How about you show me your car, huh?"

Kellen blinked once then twice before looking at Joshlyn. Slowly she felt the rage inside settle enough where she could think straight. "Um, yeah. It's, uh, over here."

Kellen took one last look at Billy before turning and walking away. She didn't say another word until they approached her tent and car.

"Listen, Joshlyn, I'm really sorry you had to see that," Kellen said with a shaky voice. Clenching her jaws, she continued. "I'm not usually like that, but that man sets me on edge and makes me angrier than I've ever been."

Joshlyn followed Kellen over to a couple chairs and waited for her to sit down. "We all have things that make us vulnerable, Kellen. Don't apologize for your feelings."

"I know, it's just that I hate that I let him get to me and that you had to see me so out of control."

Joshlyn put her hands on the arms of the chair and squatted down in front of Kellen. "Trust me, Kellen; you are not the first person I've seen out of control. Don't worry about it."

Kellen stared into Joshlyn's eyes, hoping she truly did understand. Slowly she nodded her head even though she wasn't completely convinced. "All right."

"So, this is your car, huh?" Joshlyn asked as she stood up.

Kellen stood and walked over to her car. It was bright yellow with a navy number thirteen on it.

"This would be her." Kellen grinned.

Joshlyn walked closer, ran her hand over the top, and peeked inside the window.

"Hey, how come there's only one seat in there?"

"Because only one person can drive the car at a time." Kellen laughed.

Joshlyn shook her head and chuckled. "I don't know what I expected. I should have taken a closer look that first day when Ami brought me down."

"Well, you seemed a little distracted at the time."

"Oh, and like you don't even know what that was about, do you?" Joshlyn teased.

Kellen smiled, but didn't say anything more. She loved this playful side of Joshlyn. It was nice to see her out of her shell and having a good time.

"Well, hello there, ladies," Bob said as he paused at the tent flap. He wasn't sure if he was interrupting anything or not.

Kellen turned and gestured for Bob to come closer. "Hey, Bob. This is Joshlyn Davis. Joshlyn, this is Bob Landers, my crew chief."

"Hello, Mr. Landers. It's really nice to meet you," Joshlyn said, shaking Bob's hand.

"Oh, just call me Bob, young lady. Mr. Landers is my papa's name."

Joshlyn smiled. "All right then, Bob. Kellen talks very highly of you. She says you're the best crew chief around."

"Whooeeee, what are you gonna have to pay her after this one, Kellen?" Bob said, chuckling.

Kellen rolled her eyes. "She came up with that one all her own, Bob. All kidding aside though, you are the best."

Bob blushed at Kellen's high praise and changed the subject. "You better get a move on, kiddo, if you plan to qualify for the race."

"Right. Joshlyn's going to take some pictures and hang out with us today. That okay with you?"

"Absolutely. I'll be the envy of all the guys," Bob said, tucking a thumb in his pants loop.

Kellen stepped closer to Joshlyn and put a hand on her elbow. "I hate to leave you now, but I need to go do time trials. As soon as they are done I'll have time to hang out some before the race starts."

Joshlyn looped her arm through Bob's. "Don't worry about me. I've got the best chaperone. Go on, I'll be okay."

"You can take whatever pictures you'd like, just be sure to stay behind the pit wall, okay?"

"You bet," Joshlyn assured her. "Be careful."

Kellen leaned closed and gave Joshlyn a whisper of a kiss. "Always."

After Kellen left to get ready, Joshlyn went about readying her cameras. She pulled her favorite digital camera out and checked the battery. The beauty of a digital was that you could snap all the pictures you wanted and erase the bad ones later. Her Mark III was no slouch. The self-cleaning sensor and five frames per second shooting speed were just a couple reasons she absolutely loved this camera. She grabbed a can of air out of her bag to clean her six hundred four point oh long lens, wide-angle lens, and macro lens so they were ready for later. Now she was ready to go. Gradually she started taking pictures. She snapped a few of the car before Kellen had to take it for the time trials. Joshlyn kept it to the forefront of her mind to watch out for cables and cords for she seemingly always got lost in her work. The price of her equipment alone was well worth the insurance policy she took out on it.

Joshlyn lowered the camera when Kellen came out to get in her car. This time she was dressed in a yellow jumpsuit with matching gloves and boots. In her research online, she found that the material on the jumpsuits, gloves, and boots were made of a fire-resistant material. Joshlyn raised the camera and snapped several more pictures.

Kellen smiled for the camera and then raised her helmet. With one last grin at Joshlyn, she pulled her long hair up and slid the helmet over her head.

"Here kiddo, better put these on for now," Bob said, handing Joshlyn a pair of protective headphones.

Joshlyn pulled them on just as Kellen ignited the engine. The loud rumble from the car still made her jump.

Kellen gave a thumbs up as she rolled away from

the tent towards the track. She winked as she passed Joshlyn and gave the car a little gas.

Kellen glanced in the rear-view mirror and saw Joshlyn raise her camera once again. She smiled to herself. *Damn, she's beautiful!*

❧❧❧❧

After time trials were over, Kellen pulled the car back around to her tent. The crew helped her park and then raised the hood so the engine could cool down. Kellen pulled herself up and out of the car. As soon as her feet hit the ground, she reached up to remove her helmet. Pulling it off, she shook her head so her hair would fall free around her shoulders. She raised an arm and rubbed it across her forehead. Kellen glanced around, trying to spot Joshlyn and found her off to the side, snapping pictures of none other than herself.

Joshlyn lowered the camera to stare at Kellen. *Lord have mercy! I need a cold shower just watching her get out of the car!*

Joshlyn grinned and walked over to where Kellen stood. "Hey there, how'd it go?"

"I think it went well. They should be bringing times by here pretty soon. What have you been up to?"

"Oh, you know, a little of this and a little of that."

Kellen smiled at Joshlyn's flippant remark. "Oh, really? Well, how about we get a bite to eat real quick before the race starts."

"Sounds good to me," Joshlyn replied. She reached to turn her camera off, but took one last glance at the picture in the frame before doing so. *I hope that picture turns out half as good as it looks here!*

Joshlyn stowed her gear and followed Kellen

out the back tent flap and over to some tables where several coolers sat.

"Help yourself. Drinks are usually in the cooler on the end there," Kellen pointed.

Joshlyn grabbed a bottle of water and a pre-made sandwich and followed Kellen to another bench.

They sat quietly and ate their light meal. When they finished, Kellen took their trash and tossed it in the trash barrel. She sat back down, but this time straddled the bench and faced Joshlyn.

"Was it terribly boring waiting for time trials to get over?"

Joshlyn took a sip of water before replying. "Not at all. You would not believe all the pictures I got. I find it all very fascinating, Kellen."

"Good. I was afraid you'd be bored to tears."

"I do have a question for you though."

Kellen cocked her head slightly. "What's that?"

At that angle, Joshlyn could see Kellen's eyes without any shadows or sun causing her to squint. Her eyes had a slight almond shape to them and the irises were big and colorful. When she smiled, slight little lines creased the corners.

"Joshlyn?"

"Sorry," Joshlyn said, shaking her head. "What did you say again?"

"Actually, you were the one asking. You said you had a question?"

"Oh, right…yeah, ummm…Oh, those two women wearing the really short shorts next to Emerson's tent?"

Kellen nodded and laughed. "Yep, pit lizards!"

Joshlyn laughed with Kellen and kept chuckling until Bob brought Kellen's time slip over and handed it to her.

"Here ya go. Not bad placement today. It's gonna be a hot one, though so watch yourself out there and holler if you need to," Bob said. He tipped his hat and walked back towards the tent.

"Not bad placement, but not good either."

Joshlyn glanced at the paper and saw that Kellen was starting in fifth for this race. She looked back up to Kellen only to find her chewing on a lower lip.

"Why is it not good?"

"It puts me starting right next to Billy," Kellen said with a frown.

Chapter Nine

Kellen waited patiently behind the pace car and tried in vain not to look to her right. She knew Billy would be there. No doubt he'd be looking right at her. As soon as the green flag flew, her goal was to get out fast and get away from him as soon as she could. The more distance the better.

The pace car pulled off and the green flag waved. Kellen put the hammer down and around the first turn got under the number four car in position. As long as she could keep a car length between her and Billy, she felt she'd be better off.

Kellen thought back two years ago to the accident and wished there was something she could have done. Maybe that's why she felt so outraged by Billy's actions. She watched him take pit road without slowing down. It all seemed surreal as she watched him plow into the back end of another car, pushing it directly into Kellen's crew. Most of them made it back over the wall, but Peetie never had a chance. She exited her car as quick as she could, but Peetie died almost instantly. The look on Billy's face was one she'd never forget. He looked her right in the eyes, raised an eyebrow, and shrugged. In her heart, she felt Billy did it on purpose. He showed no remorse and in the end claimed engine failure.

"How do pieces of shit like that live with themselves," Kellen murmured.

Mind on your task, Kellen! Think of what's waiting for you at the end.

Kellen grinned and gunned the car once more.

✿✿✿✿

Joshlyn snapped photo after photo until her arms needed a rest. She walked over to Bob and bumped his arm with her shoulder.

"How's she doing?"

"She's doing great. Driving with a vengeance if you ask me," Bob said.

"You can tell that from here?"

"I can tell because I've watched her race many, many times. She never gets out that fast and so early in the race."

"Maybe it's better that she does. From where I'm sitting, the further from Billy she is, the better."

Bob chuckled. "I couldn't agree with you more, little lady. I tell you what; there isn't any other person I know that gets her that fired up that quick."

"Sounds like he's deserving though. Do you really think he had engine failure?"

"Between you, me, and the higher power? No, I don't think he had engine failure. Billy Baker has had it in for Kellen for a long time."

"Old history between them?"

"Actually, it's old history between their fathers. See, Kellen's pa was an old dru—" Bob stopped abruptly.

"It's okay, Bob. She's already told me about her father."

Bob nodded and continued. "Her pa was an old drunk and he never did right by anybody. That includes Billy's pa, Bill Sr. They were out drinking one night and Jeff, that's Kellen's pa, started spouting off. They got into this huge fight in the middle of the bar and both of them got kicked out."

"Does Kellen know this story?"

"Oh yeah, she's the one that had to go bail Jeff out of jail afterwards."

Joshlyn nodded and waited for him to continue.

"Anyhow, they continued to fight in the parking lot and damaged several cars. Bill Sr. grabbed a ball bat out of the back of a truck and started taking shots at Jeff. By this time, the cops showed up and took them both to jail."

"It's a wonder neither one of them got hurt up to this point."

"Oh, they both took their turns and had plenty of bruises to show for it, but neither was seriously injured. Kellen showed up and bailed Jeff out, but Bill's wife, Wanda, refused. She said she'd had enough and he could find his own way out this time."

"Ouch!"

"Yep, but you know, he deserved it and so did Jeff. He should have kept his butt in jail that night, too."

"Why didn't he?" Joshlyn asked.

"Kellen got tired of the calls. She was going to let him sober up, but he kept calling. Finally, she went and bailed him out, and told him to leave her alone. It wasn't long after that he tried to rob one of the convenience stores, shot a clerk, and ended up behind bars for a long time. Wouldn't you know that he blames her for that?"

Joshlyn didn't say a word, but her dropped jaw said plenty.

"He's a right old son of a bitch, Joshlyn."

"That's insane! So, what happened to Bill?"

"By the time Bill got out of jail, Wanda had already packed her stuff and left. Three days later they found Bill in his truck with a bullet in his head."

"Wow. That's terrible. So, does Billy blame Jeff for his father's death?"

"You know, I reckon he does. He hasn't come right out and said so, but he's had this vendetta against Kellen ever since. If that's not blame then I don't know what is."

"That doesn't make sense, Bob. Why would he have a vendetta against Kellen? I mean, none of that was her doing."

"I'm not rightly sure, but I'm guessing it's because she's the only one around to take his frustration and blame out on."

"Hmm," Joshlyn murmured. "What about Wanda?"

"Nobody's heard from her since; not even Billy."

Joshlyn shook her head. "It's sad, for all of them involved."

"That it is, my dear. Now it's time to pay attention to the race. You might want to get your camera back out because the finish is coming up. They are three laps from the end and trust me, you don't want to miss this finish," Bob said with a huge grin.

Joshlyn grabbed her camera again, snapped her long lens in place, and waited patiently to see what was going to happen.

❧ ❧ ❧ ❧

Kellen felt the adrenaline kick in and tightened

her hands on the steering wheel. Three laps to go and she was in second place now. She glanced in her mirror and saw Billy coming up behind her. She pushed to full throttle and pulled away a little. She knew that with the down force on this short track she could be a little more aggressive without having drastic results. She hugged the curb around the corner and hit the pedal again.

"I got my eyes on you, Billy!" Kellen screamed. She knew he couldn't hear her, but it made her feel better to vocalize her thoughts. "You're not getting by me today and that's a promise."

Kellen's eyes shot to her rear view mirror when she felt her car jerk. Billy was right up against her bumper, tapping her. She weaved a little, trying to get him off her. They were on the straightaway now, heading for the second turn that would take them to the white flag. Kellen put her foot down again and took the corner as fast as she could. She could see the white flag flying and set her mind for the last lap.

"What the hell…you bastard," Kellen whispered as she watched Billy come right up on her bumper again. He tapped her again, causing the car to pull towards the wall. Kellen pulled the wheel towards her to get back in line again.

The two cars bumped and shifted down the first straight away and into the first turn. Billy tried once again to close in, but Kellen shook out of it quick and didn't give him a chance to clip her car again. As they started to round the next corner, Kellen kept one eye on the road and the other on Billy.

"C'mon you son of a bitch. You want to play? Bring it on!"

There wasn't much room between Kellen and

the number one car and if she planned it right, she had an idea that just might work.

Kellen watched as Billy drew closer. As they came out of the final turn, she knew he was waiting to bump her again. She took her foot off the gas pedal slightly and when Billy went for the bump, she beat him to it.

Kellen bumped the front of Billy's car and hit the gas at the same time. When they came out of the corner, Kellen shot in front of the number one car and came down the straight away.

⁂

"Holy shit!" Bob exclaimed.

Joshlyn continued taking pictures, but lowered the camera after Kellen bumped Billy's car. She watched as Billy's car slammed sideways into the fence and Kellen overtook the lead car.

With scant inches to spare, Kellen took the checkered flag.

Bob jumped up and down and grabbed Joshlyn in a big bear hug. His excitement bubbled over and Joshlyn found herself laughing and crying at the same time.

"I can't believe it! I just can't believe it!"

"Bob, I can't breathe!" Joshlyn forced out.

Bob released her but kept an arm over her shoulders. "Oh, sorry. Wow, what a race! She'd sure make her grandpappa proud today."

Joshlyn could see the pride beaming in Bob's smile. He couldn't have been happier if Kellen was his own granddaughter. Joshlyn suspected that Bob probably considered her kin as it were.

"Has she ever won a race before, Bob?"

"Of course she's won races before, but never in the fashion that she won this one today. Did you see that move she put on Billy?"

"I saw it, but I have to admit that I don't really know what happened."

Bob gave a big belly laugh. "She put a lesson on that boy today. One I'm sure he won't soon forget either."

Joshlyn laughed and celebrated with Kellen's crew while she waited for Kellen to make her way back over to the pit.

⁂

Kellen whooped and hollered as she flew past the finish line. "Yes! Yes! Yes!" She yelled and pumped a fist. She took her victory lap and pulled back onto pit road. She couldn't wait to see her crew and Joshlyn. She wasn't even concerned about Billy. He got what was coming to him. Kellen was certain he wasn't hurt because of how his car hit the fence. However, it was enough to let him know she meant business and he had better find someone else to mess with.

One of Kellen's crewmembers lowered the netting on her window and helped her out of the car. She pulled her helmet off and was immediately swarmed. Back slaps and hugs followed and she could hear a cork pop somewhere.

Kellen removed her gloves and looked over the heads of the people around her. She knew Joshlyn had to be here somewhere. Feeling a hand on her shoulder, she turned abruptly. She was prepared to face Billy head on should she need to. Instead, she found herself looking into the warmth of Joshlyn's beautiful eyes.

"Congrats, hot shot," Joshlyn said with a smile.

"Why thank you, my lady," Kellen said as she leaned in to give Joshlyn a hug.

"That was the most amazing thing I've ever seen, Kellen."

Kellen blushed and wet her lips with her tongue. *Why on earth was she feeling like a schoolgirl with a crush?*

Joshlyn pulled Kellen in for another hug and placed a kiss against her ear. She took a deep breath of courage and spoke in a soft tone. "You think you might be interested in another victory lap after you take me home?"

Chapter Ten

Kellen's stomach felt like there were a hundred butterflies floating around in it. She was more than ready to take the relationship with Joshlyn further, but knowing it was within reach made her nervous as all get out. It felt like this moment would never arrive. The post-race interviews and celebrations seemed to take forever and making it worse was the fact that Joshlyn was right there watching every word she said and every movement she made. Finally, the last interview was over and Kellen couldn't get away fast enough.

Now, walking up the sidewalk to Joshlyn's house, all she wanted was Joshlyn in her arms.

Joshlyn glanced over her shoulder at Kellen as she unlocked the front door. She smiled and pushed it open, waiting for Kellen to enter.

Kellen walked slowly through the door without taking her eyes off Joshlyn's.

After closing the door, Joshlyn turned to Kellen.

"Would you like something to drink?" She asked, placing a hand on Kellen's arm.

"Sure," Kellen nodded.

Joshlyn slid her hand down Kellen's arm and started past her.

Kellen's eyes followed Joshlyn's hand as it moved down her arm. When her fingers briefly closed over hers, Kellen curled her hand and pulled Joshlyn to a stop.

"I'm, uh, not really thirsty…for, uh…" Kellen stumbled for the right words, stopped to take a deep breath, and then continued. "I don't need anything to drink, Joshlyn. I just need you."

Joshlyn could see the longing in Kellen's eyes and took a small unperceivable step towards her. Knotting her hands in the front of Kellen's shirt, she pulled her closer. Joshlyn lay her head against Kellen's chest and felt her heart pounding against her cheek. She smiled to herself and turned her face to take in the leather and spice scent of Kellen's shirt. It was a different smell than Joshlyn was used to, but assumed it was from the leather suit that Kellen wore while driving.

"I should probably take a shower," Kellen whispered.

"I like the way you smell."

Kellen was trembling and hoped in vain that Joshlyn wouldn't notice. She was driving her crazy with the nuzzling and the soft touches. What she really wanted was for Joshlyn to throw her down and make mad passionate all night love to her.

"You're shaking," Joshlyn said, raising her eyes to Kellen's.

"Mmm, yeah. You tend to do that to me," Kellen responded.

Joshlyn slid a hand up Kellen's chest and then behind her neck and pulled her in close. She leaned forward at the same time and placed her lips against Kellen's. The slow, soft kiss Joshlyn started with evolved quickly into a fiery ball of untethered nerves waiting to explode.

Breaking the kiss, Kellen leaned her forehead against Joshlyn's. "You are driving me insane, Joshlyn."

Joshlyn glanced up at Kellen and licked her lower lip. "Then the feeling is mutual."

"Yeah?" Kellen asked.

"Oh, yeah."

"How about you tel—" Kellen stopped abruptly as Joshlyn put a finger to her lips.

"No more talking, Kellen. Show me…show me how you feel," Joshlyn said, removing her finger.

Kellen grabbed Joshlyn's arm and pulled her against her chest. She lowered her head and took Joshlyn's mouth with desperate need. She slid her hands up under the back edge of Joshlyn's shirt and stroked the bare, warm flesh under her fingers. Moving her hands up and around to the front of Joshlyn's chest, she cupped both breasts and squeezed gently.

Joshlyn moaned and started backing them both towards her bedroom. The last thing she wanted was to be rolling around on the floor like two sex-starved teenagers, but God help her, if they didn't get there fast, that is exactly what they'd be doing.

Kellen stopped Joshlyn in the hall and pushed her back against the wall. She laced both of Joshlyn's hands in hers and raised them above her head. She placed a leg between Joshlyn's thighs and stepped close, grinding her hip against Joshlyn's pelvis.

Joshlyn tilted her head back submissively as Kellen's mouth ravaged her throat, neck, and ear.

"Is this what you want, Joshlyn?"

"Yes, God, yes," Joshlyn whimpered in a hoarse voice.

Kellen's stomach tightened and her blood ran hotter. She took Joshlyn's hand and led the rest of the way into the bedroom. She stopped short of the bed and started unbuttoning Joshlyn's shirt.

Joshlyn caught her lower lip between her teeth as the last button came loose. She gave the window a cursory glance as the material slipped off her shoulders. She let the shirt fall free and then reached over to slip Kellen's shirt over her head.

In seconds, both of them had removed their clothing. Joshlyn pulled Kellen down on top of her and kissed her as a new surge of sexual energy swirled deep in her gut. She buried her nose in Kellen's neck, not caring about the musky scent of sweat on her skin. Never had she wanted someone as much as she wanted Kellen. She was scared of the transition in their relationship, but the need and want of this physical intimacy outweighed her fears. The only thing that could put a damper at this point would be if Kellen weren't ready.

Joshlyn nipped the soft surface with her teeth and slid her hands into Kellen's hair to hold her still so she could see her face.

"Are you okay with this, Kellen?"

"I'm definitely okay; more than okay actually," Kellen said, grinning.

Joshlyn nodded and placed her hands against Kellen's chest. She gave a slight push, making Kellen sit up astride her. Once she was there, Joshlyn slid her hands down to cup her breasts. She kneaded them gently before taking each nipple between her fingers. Joshlyn elicited a deep moan from Kellen as she brought her hips up and squeezed her nipples at the same time.

"Fuck, Joshlyn, you're going to make me come if you do that again." Kellen felt ready to explode as it was and knew it wouldn't take much to send her over the edge.

"Go ahead, Kellen, there's no need to hold back.

We've got all night long," Joshlyn responded, rolling her hips for punctuation.

Kellen leaned down and took a nipple between her lips. Flicking it with her tongue, she pushed her hips down against Joshlyn's. She continued to suck and nibble on Joshlyn's nipple as she moved a hand between them. She slipped her fingers on each side of Joshlyn's clit and moved them through the silken wetness.

"Oh, my God…Oh, Kellen!"

"That's it, baby; move with me…let it go," Kellen whispered as she slid both fingers deep inside. She hadn't intended to turn the tables on Joshlyn, but the need to touch her was overwhelming. The soft, sensual moans and unmistakable, musky scent of excitement pushed her beyond the point of simply wanting Joshlyn. She needed her.

"Oh, God, I'm so close…" Joshlyn moaned, moving faster against Kellen's stroking fingers.

"Good, baby…just let it go," Kellen purred.

Joshlyn arched her back up off the bed and gasped as her body exploded. Her toes curled as her center throbbed and she felt like she was floating in a million pieces.

Kellen leaned down and kissed Joshlyn. "You are an incredible woman, Josh."

"And you, Reynolds, play dirty pool," Joshlyn said as she rolled Kellen to her back.

"What?"

Joshlyn grinned down at her, knowing full well Kellen was aware of what she'd done.

"Now it's my turn, you little trouble maker." Joshlyn curled her fingers in Kellen's and placed them by her head as she leaned down and dropped butterfly kisses over Kellen's forehead, then her eyes, down to her nose, on her chin, and lastly the moist parted lips awaiting her. She nipped first at the upper lip and then sucked Kellen's lower lip in her mouth. Releasing it, Joshlyn moved slowly down her body, leaving a trail of moist kisses behind her. When she reached the apex between Kellen's legs, she ran her hands, palm side up, along the inside of her thighs and spread her legs gently.

Kellen's breath quickened as her legs opened, giving Joshlyn full access to whatever she wanted. A white-hot bolt of electricity shot through her core when Joshlyn's lips and tongue touched her.

"Oh, Josh, that feels so good," Kellen moaned.

Joshlyn ran her tongue up over Kellen's clit and back down. Each time she did, Kellen twitched and jumped. She knew Kellen was about to orgasm and wanted to hold it off a little longer.

"You like that, do you?"

"Please, don't stop…please," Kellen begged.

Joshlyn couldn't bring herself to hold off any longer, not when Kellen was begging. She took the engorged clit between her lips, slid two fingers deep inside, and started a slow stroke. The closer Kellen got to the edge the faster she stroked until finally she sent her over.

Kellen bucked beneath Joshlyn's mouth and hands and then her body went taut as a rush of molten heat spilled from within her.

"Oh, God, baby, that was…"

"I know, believe me, I know."

Joshlyn moved up beside Kellen and gathered her into her arms. Kellen curled around Joshlyn and closed her eyes.

Chapter Eleven

Kellen slowly became aware of her surroundings. Joshlyn's warm, supple body was wrapped over and around Kellen's entire left side. She had a protective arm thrown across Kellen's waist and her face snuggled into the crook of her neck.

Kellen tightened her hold. She could definitely get used to waking up like this. It was early, that much she knew even though the blinds were pulled closed. She glanced at the clock on the bedside table. Four forty-five in the morning. Chigger would need to be let out very soon. He was a good dog, but even good dogs could only hold it for so long.

"Why are you awake already?"

"How did you know I was awake?" Kellen asked.

"I could feel you thinking," Joshlyn mumbled.

Kellen grinned and kissed Joshlyn on the top of her head. "I've got to get up and go, sweetheart."

Joshlyn groaned. Leaning up on an elbow, she kissed Kellen on the lips. "Do you have to go so soon?"

"I don't want to, but Chigger might disagree."

Joshlyn crossed her arms on Kellen's chest and rested her chin on them. "Ah, well, I don't want to upset Chigger. He's my in."

Kellen ran her hand through Joshlyn's hair, clasped a piece between her fingers, and tugged gently. "As if..."

"Yeah?"

Kellen drew Joshlyn down. "Oh, yeah," she said and closed her lips over Joshlyn's.

The kiss started tentatively at first, but gained momentum in a span of a few seconds. Joshlyn shifted slightly so she was on top of Kellen and slid a leg between her thighs. Her tongue pressed for entrance and met no resistance.

Kellen's hands were all over Joshlyn. She couldn't get enough, but knew they had to stop or she'd never get home.

"Baby, I really, *really* want to continue this, but I better go before the getting's no good."

Joshlyn sighed, but acquiesced. "I know...I know." She flopped on her back and sighed again. "I can't seem to get enough of you. What have you done to me?"

Everything about Kellen pulled at Joshlyn's senses. Her smell, her touch, the way she responded to the littlest things. She was smart as hell and gave as good as she got.

"I don't think it's anything you haven't already done to me." Kellen laughed.

Joshlyn laughed with her. "Point taken," she said, rolling up and out of bed. "Come on, up with you then. Get out of my bed before I keep you there forever."

Kellen took the offered hand and crawled out of bed. She held Joshlyn close, reveling in the moment. Nothing compared to a little post coital bliss.

Joshlyn ran her fingers lightly down Kellen's cheek. "Do you want to take a shower before you leave?"

Kellen leaned into the touch. "I'll take one when I get home. After I get Chigger taken care of and shower, would it be okay to come back over? Maybe we could go for breakfast and coffee?"

"I'd like that. Just come over when you're ready. I'll be here."

Kellen stared deep into Joshlyn's eyes. Something seemed a little off or out of place and then Joshlyn blinked. Kellen continued to stare until Joshlyn spoke.

"Go. The sooner you do the sooner you can come back."

Kellen nodded and turned to get dressed.

᠎᠎᠎᠎᠎᠎᠎᠎◈◈◈◈

After Kellen left, Joshlyn hopped in the shower. Lathering her hair and soaping her body, she thought back on the night. Kellen had awoken and they made love again and again until they were both satiated and worn out. Joshlyn couldn't remember a night that she enjoyed more or gave so freely. Even prior to three years ago, she'd never shared this kind of passion with anyone. Hell, she'd never felt this kind of passion before. The emotions consumed her and she was hell bent on exploring every feeling she possessed.

Joshlyn stepped out of the shower and dried. Wrapping the towel around her, she glanced in the mirror. She tilted her head back and put some eye drops in her eyes. Leaning closer to the mirror, she blinked a few times. Kellen was very perceptive and Joshlyn was afraid they were about to have their first heartfelt conversation until she was able to distract her.

"That was close…too close," Joshlyn said to her reflection.

Joshlyn left the bathroom and pulled some

clothes on. She padded down the hall to her office and plopped down in the chair in front of her desk. She turned on her computer, pulled her camera from the bag, and removed the memory card.

"Let's take a look at these babies and see if we got any good ones."

Joshlyn clicked on the icon to open the program she used for her pictures and then opened up the folder of new pictures she took at the race. She quickly scanned the pictures for the one of Kellen removing her helmet and leaned back when it popped up on her monitor.

"Wow, she is absolutely stunning." Joshlyn stared at the picture. The smile and twinkle in Kellen's eyes looked like it was meant just for her.

Joshlyn clicked her mouse a few times and then hit the print button. She continued clicking and printing until she'd worked through the entire folder.

❧ ❧ ❧ ❧

Kellen stepped through the door and greeted an excited Chigger. He was wiggling and jumping circles around her.

"Hey there boy, did you miss me?"

Kellen set her stuff on the kitchen table and squatted. "Who's a good boy? Hmm? Is that you?"

Kellen scratched the pooch's head and then let him outside. She filled his bowls with water and food and walked into the living room to click on the television. She glanced around the room and for the first time realized how empty it really felt. There was nothing personal about the room. It could have been anyone's living room and for that reason alone Kellen felt sad. This was supposed to be her home, her haven. It didn't seem to matter before, but now she wanted it to. Having someone special in her life gave Kellen a different perspective on the important things and she vowed to make some changes.

Chigger pawing at the sliding glass door brought Kellen back to the kitchen. She let the pup in and headed for the shower.

Opting for a tub of hot, bubbly water instead of a shower, Kellen climbed in and sank up to her shoulders. She laid her head back against the edge of the tub and closed her eyes. There were muscles in her body that hadn't ached like this in quite a while. *Not that I'm complaining in the least!* Joshlyn took her to the brink and dropped her over it many times throughout the night.

"Joshlyn, God, what you do to me," Kellen murmured. Sitting here soaking wasn't going to get her back to the one person she really wanted to see. She grabbed a Loofa and squeezed some bath gel onto it. Lathering her arms and legs, she pulled the plug on the tub and stood. She turned the shower nozzle on, shampooed and conditioned her hair, and rinsed off.

Kellen dried and dressed and was heading back down the hall to the living room when she heard her name on the television.

"*...local stock car driver, Kellen Reynolds, pulls off the upset victory in last night's Amateur I-70 Series. Here with an interview directly following that win is TV9's own Melissa Stewart.*"

"*Thanks, Dave. Last night here at the I-70 Speedway we had an outstanding turn out for the Amateur Series. It was a heated battle, but in the end, the number thirteen Monte Carlo driven by Kellen*

*Reynolds took the checkered flag. Here is what Ms.
Reynolds had to say last night…"*

"Wow, I made the local news," Kellen said,
amused.

❧ ❧ ❧ ❧

Joshlyn was clipping the last photos up to dry
when the phone rang. Snapping her gloves off, she
hurried into the living room and grabbed the phone.

"Hello?"

"Hey there. Whatcha doin', hot stuff?"

Joshlyn laughed. "Hey, Ami, I was printing off
some pictures and waiting for Kellen to come back
over. What are you up to?"

"You might want to turn your television on to
channel nine. Your Ms. Wonderful's interview from
last night is on."

Joshlyn grabbed the remote and clicked on the
television. Changing the channel, she caught the tail
end of the interview.

*"…Who do you attribute your talent to, Ms.
Reynolds?"*

*"I couldn't do all this without the help of my crew
and I've got the best crew chief in Bob Landers. It also
helps to have a special someone waiting for you at the
finish line."*

Joshlyn watched Kellen look directly into the
camera. She'd know that sparkle in her eye anywhere
and smiled.

"Anything else you'd like to say, Ms. Reynolds?"

*"That's it, Melissa. I'm ready to go celebrate with
my crew and friends."*

"Thank you for the interview, Ms.—"

"It's Kellen, please."

"All right. Thank you for the interview, Kellen. We look forward to seeing more of your driving in the future."

"Thank you."

"Dave, back to you."

"What a great interview."

"I'll say. That's a great girl you got there, Joshlyn. I'd say you better hang on to her. She seems pretty smitten over you."

"You think so, huh?"

"Honey, you and I both know she was talking about you at the end of that interview." Ami chuckled. "Seriously though, she really seems to be taken with you."

"Well, the feeling is mutual, Ami. I'm almost afraid to see where this is going to go."

"Now, Josh, don't start questioning the relationship. Just let things happen and go with the flow."

Joshlyn grinned. "I said almost, Ami."

Ami and Joshlyn talked a little longer before Joshlyn finally said she had to go. Kellen should be returning any time and she wanted to be ready.

As Joshlyn hung up the phone, she noticed her message light blinking. Tapping the button, she waited for the message to play.

"Joshlyn, this is Sydney. I know it's been awhile since we last spoke, but it's urgent that I get in touch with you. Please give me a call as soon as you get this message. My number is—"

Joshlyn stopped the message abruptly and sank to the floor. "Not now, please not now," she whispered.

Chapter Twelve

Kellen pulled up in front of Joshlyn's house and sat there for a moment. Turning the SUV off, she palmed the keys. It was hard to believe what was happening between them. She wanted it, no doubt, but things in her life didn't seem that attainable most times, especially not something she wanted as much as she wanted Joshlyn. Sure, she had her own business, but that was different. Work was something she always found easy to get lost in and never really had to work that hard at doing. This was most definitely different. Relationships were never easy, at least not in Kellen's experience. Eventually someone would pinch her and she'd wake up to find this all for naught.

Kellen squeezed the keys in her hand, making the pointed edges dig into her flesh. She glanced down and grinned at the indentions she found. This was definitely real and Joshlyn was just beyond the front door, waiting for her. Kellen leaned over and grabbed the local paper and a small bouquet of flowers she picked up on the way back over to Joshlyn's. She exited the SUV and strolled casually up the walk to the front door. She was almost there when the door opened and Joshlyn leaned against the door jam and smiled in her direction. Kellen stumbled slightly and then stopped all together. *It should be illegal for her to stand there with that saucy grin on her face, knowing exactly what it does to me!*

Kellen cleared her throat. "Stop that."

"Excuse me?" Joshlyn said with a chuckle.

"You heard me, you tease," Kellen stated, continuing her walk to the front door.

"I have absolutely no clue what you are referring to."

Kellen stopped in front of Joshlyn and tilted her head. Seeing Joshlyn's smirk affirmed that she did indeed know what Kellen was talking about.

"You may think that smile and charm will work on someone else, but it certainly won't work on me," Kellen challenged.

"Oh really?" Joshlyn asked, stepping as close to her as she could without actually touching her. She ran a finger lightly up the buttons on Kellen's white, sleeveless shirt and tapped her chin. "Somehow I doubt that if I really wanted to charm you that you'd be able to resist."

Kellen was about to respond when Joshlyn ran her finger back down her shirt and continued on down the zipper of her shorts. She opened her palm and cupped Kellen briefly before sliding her fingers back up the front of her shorts, flicking the button.

Kellen gulped audibly, wrapped her arms around Joshlyn, and shoved her back through the door, kicking it closed with her foot.

"Sweetheart, I hope you didn't start something you aren't ready to finish."

"Oh, trust me, we've only just begun," Joshlyn hummed in her ear as she pulled Kellen to the floor.

❧ ❧ ❧ ❧

Kellen tucked her shirt back inside her shorts

and clasped the small belt buckle. She retrieved the flowers from their spot on the chair and handed them to Joshlyn, who was just finishing dressing herself.

"Since I didn't get the chance to give these to you earlier, beautiful flowers for a beautiful woman."

"Oh, Kellen, they're gorgeous," Joshlyn said, sniffing the fragrant buds. "That was really sweet of you. Thank you."

Kellen placed her hand against the side of Joshlyn's face and let her thumb graze over the smooth surface of her cheek. "You are more than welcome. Thank you for a wonderful evening and afternoon. You can't possibly know what this has all meant to me, Joshlyn."

Joshlyn cleared her throat, turned her head, and kissed the thumb stroking lightly against her skin. She tilted her head, catching the hand between her cheek and shoulder and squeezed gently. "As much as you can't possibly know what it means to me, Kellen."

"So..." Kellen trailed off.

"So, oh, hang on just a second." Joshlyn turned and ran down the hall to her office.

Joshlyn grabbed the small packet of pictures off her desk and held them against her chest. She took a deep breath before going back down the hall to Kellen.

"I took these at the race, I hope you like them," Joshlyn said, tentatively handing the pictures over to Kellen.

Kellen opened the package and pulled the pictures out all in one grouping. She glanced at the first one and felt the air leave her lungs. How had Joshlyn managed to make her look so good in that hideous race suit? One by one, she worked through the pictures, each one just as amazing as the first. There was a clear shot from the front of the car as Kellen came off a turn and another of her coming down pit row. A couple of her standing by the car clearly captured the love she held for racing. Her hand resting on the car, the helmet under her arm, and the grin on her face drew her into the picture. She felt like she was standing there again, the ever-present butterflies winding their way through her stomach and the adrenaline coursing through her veins just waiting for the race to start.

"Joshlyn, I…I don't even know what to say." Kellen shook her head. "These are amazing. You have a great eye." Kellen glanced at the pictures and looked back up. Softly she spoke directly from her heart. "Thank you."

Joshlyn released the breath she was holding. "You're welcome. I was hoping you'd like them."

"I love them. Maybe while we are out we could get some frames?"

"Sure. Do you know where you'd like to hang them?" Joshlyn asked.

"Well, I thought maybe in the living room on that wall that is so bare. What do you think?"

"I think that sounds like a perfect spot."

Kellen smiled and offered an arm. "Shall we get started then, my lady?"

"We shall. Lead on, my dear." Joshlyn smiled in return.

❧❧❧❧

Joshlyn ran her hands over the oak frame. It was a little more expensive than the others, but the quality was more than worth it. It would look perfect in combination to Kellen's entertainment center.

After a relaxing breakfast in a quaint little nook that Kellen knew about, they decided to walk down to the frame and photo shop. Joshlyn really enjoyed spending time with Kellen. Conversation flowed easily and when they weren't talking, the silence was not uncomfortable in the least. She glanced over to where Kellen was standing and studied her unabashedly. The small buttons running down the front of her shirt about drove Joshlyn insane earlier. She was so turned on and the buttons weren't cooperating. She had to rein herself in from just ripping the shirt open and the buttons be damned! Kellen was one sexy woman who could make her blood boil with just a look. *I'm just lucky that I seem to have the same effect on her!*

"Hey, Kel," Joshlyn waited for Kellen to turn her way. "What do you think of these?" Joshlyn didn't even think when she shortened Kellen's name, but when she saw the widened eyes and the stiffening of her shoulders, she made a mental note to ask her about it later.

Kellen was startled by the shortened version of her name. She hadn't heard that in…well, in a long time. By the look on Joshlyn's face, she knew that she didn't hide the reaction very well. She put the frame she was looking at back on the shelf and walked over to where Joshlyn was standing.

"They are a little more than the others, but I think they're a good quality," Joshlyn commented.

Kellen was glad that Joshlyn didn't question her reaction. She took the frame, turned it over, and looked at the front and back. "I think you're right. I'll get these. I think they'll look great with the entertainment center."

"My thoughts exactly." Joshlyn nodded, followed

Kellen up to the register to pay for the frames, and smiled at the woman behind the register.

"Oh, these frames are gorgeous and they are on sale this week. I don't think you'll be disappointed in them at all," the woman commented.

Kellen handed her card over to pay for the purchase and waited to sign the receipt. "Thank you," Kellen replied, folding the receipt and putting it in her wallet.

"Thank you. You ladies have a nice day."

"You, too," Joshlyn responded, following Kellen out the door.

They walked quietly back to the SUV and headed home with very little small talk. Joshlyn was amending her earlier thoughts about things not being tense between them when Kellen finally spoke.

"Listen, Joshlyn, about earlier, I, uh…it's been awhile since I've heard someone call me Kel and it took me by surprise." In fact, it had been twenty-three years since she'd heard it used. Honestly, she wasn't really sure how she felt about it, but knew that being an ass to Joshlyn wasn't the right thing to do. It wasn't her fault.

Joshlyn reached over and cradled her hand, rubbing her thumb over the back surface. "Hey, it's ok. I wasn't offended." Joshlyn hesitated before continuing. "Do you want to talk about it?"

"I think so…yes."

Kellen pulled up in front of Joshlyn's house and turned the vehicle off.

Joshlyn gave her hand a little tug. "Well, come on in then and we'll have some coffee and if you feel up to it we can talk about it."

"Okay," Kellen responded, getting out of the SUV.

Kellen followed Joshlyn up the walk and debated on how much she wanted to share or how much she actually could share. It wasn't an easy topic, especially since she didn't know much of the details herself.

Joshlyn unlocked the door and Kellen followed her inside.

"Have a seat, I won't be but a minute," Joshlyn said, indicating the couch.

Kellen kicked her shoes off and sat on the couch. On one hand, she could just tell Joshlyn everything she knew and hoped she understood that she probably wouldn't have all the answers to her questions. But on the other hand, was she ready *for* those questions she might not have answers to? Kellen shook her head. Either way it was going to be a frustrating situation. Kellen sighed and picked at some unseen lint on her shorts. She could hear Joshlyn moving around in the kitchen. If she really wanted to make this easy, she could just tell her some other time and make a break for it before she even came back from the kitchen. *What are you, a chickenshit, Reynolds?*

Joshlyn crossed the room from the kitchen and set a cup of coffee down on the table in front of Kellen. She set hers down and curled up on the couch facing Kellen.

"Do you feel up to talking about this?" Joshlyn asked.

Kellen sighed again and then nodded. "Might as well."

Joshlyn waited for Kellen to speak again, trying not to push her. This was apparently something Kellen had been thinking about, from what Joshlyn could tell when she came back in the room. Kellen was nervously picking at her shorts and licking her lips. Joshlyn knew the signs and Kellen was definitely displaying them. She picked up her coffee and blew at the edge of the cup before gingerly taking a sip. The hot liquid burned a path down her throat.

Kellen leaned forward and picked up her cup. Joshlyn watched the steam rise as Kellen inhaled the aroma.

Kellen spoke so softly Joshlyn almost couldn't hear her. "I don't remember a lot of details from when I was a child, but I do remember my mom always calling me Kel. I remember the first time she said it."

Joshlyn watched Kellen's eyes glaze over as she recalled the details from her childhood.

"Daddy had come home one day from work and was pissed that dinner was not already on the table…"

"God dammit! How many times do I have to tell you when I walk in that door I expect dinner to be sittin' on this table, waitin' and ready!" Jeff bellowed as the back door slammed shut.

"It's almost ready, just go get cleaned up and by the time you get back you'll be able to sit down and eat," Kellen's mom, Anne, stated.

Kellen stood in the doorway as Jeff grabbed Anne's arm and squeezed. She could tell by the wince on her momma's face that he was hurting her.

"Listen you little bitch, when I say dinner is to be on the table that's God damned well what I mean," he said, jerking her arm and then slinging it away from him.

"Jeff—" Anne started.

Jeff turned on her, getting right up in her face. "What!"

"Please, just go wash up for dinner." Her voice quivered.

Jeff brought his arm back, but before he could swing, Kellen ran into the room and wrapped herself around her momma's waist. Jeff stopped and glared at her. Leaning down, he breathed right into her face. Kellen could smell the alcohol when he came in the door, but this close up just about made her vomit.

"And you," he said, poking her in the chest. "I don't want to hear a fucking word out of you tonight."

Jeff stormed out of the room, leaving Anne and Kellen staring in his wake. Anne could feel the sobs coming from her daughter and knelt down and pulled her into her arms.

"Oh, Kel, sweetie, please don't cry. It'll be okay," she said, stroking the little girl's long hair. "You are so brave to come in here when your pa is like this."

"I didn't like seeing him hurt you, momma," Kellen sniffled.

"My little warrior," Anne cooed.

Joshlyn kept a careful eye on Kellen as she relayed the event from her past. She seemed somewhat agitated, but in control. What a horrible man her father must have been and for her to put up with it for so long. Based on what Bob had told her and the information Kellen just shared, it was no wonder Kellen turned out as well as she did. Joshlyn felt sympathy for the child Kellen was and the conditions she had survived.

Kellen shook her head and took a sip of coffee. She swallowed and licked her lips for the nth time. She glanced in Joshlyn's direction and felt relief more than anything, for there was no pity in Joshlyn's eyes. Only a quiet understanding of what Kellen's childhood must have been like. Kellen half expected a barrage of questions before she started recounting the story, but knew now that it wasn't going to happen. Joshlyn apparently did not intend to dredge up a past that was better left where it was.

"There you have it; my father in *one* of his bastardized moments."

"Does it bother you that I called you that, Kellen?"

"No...actually it was somewhat comforting. I just didn't realize it at the time."

Joshlyn scooted closer and traced the outer edge of Kellen's ear. "Good."

Kellen stared into Joshlyn's brown eyes and leaned forward. She closed her lips over Joshlyn's full ones and slowly kissed her. It wasn't a passionate kiss, but one of understanding and thankfulness.

"Thank you," Kellen whispered.

Chapter Thirteen

Joshlyn juggled the bags in her hand and pulled the keys from her pocket with the other. She could hear the phone ringing on the other side of the door as she inserted the key into the lock. Pushing the door open, she set her bags on the floor and grabbed the phone before the final ring.

"Hello," Joshlyn answered, out of breath.

"Hey there, did I catch you at a bad time?"

"Not at all, Ami, I just got home and was unlocking the door when the phone started ringing."

"Darn, and here I was hoping Kellen was the reason you were breathing so heavy." Ami laughed.

Joshlyn chuckled as she plopped down on the couch. "You are relentless; funny, but relentless."

"Yeah, well, Jaxon doesn't complain."

"Oh, that is way more information than I want to know." Joshlyn shivered.

Ami burst out laughing and Joshlyn felt her face heat up. Ami enjoyed embarrassing her any chance she got.

"So, did you call just to bust my chops or did you have something you really wanted to talk about?"

"Actually, I do have something I want to talk to you about. I don't need an answer right away, but I want you to think about it."

Ami waited for Joshlyn to respond before continuing.

Joshlyn tried to read the tone of Ami's voice to determine if this was a good something she wanted to talk about or not.

"Okay, I'm listening."

"Before you say anything, just hear me out and then I'll answer any questions you have, okay?"

"Okaaaayyy."

"Earlier today I was contacted by a freelance writer who has seen your work. She wants to do a whole series of non-fiction books and she wants you to do the pictures." Ami heard Joshlyn's quick intake of breath and rushed on.

"You would only be required to have an initial meeting and then you can correspond via email if that's what you'd like. When the project is all finished, you'll get together one last time to finalize everything. She'll give you the topics and said you'd have free rein to take whatever pictures you wanted. She's very impressed with the quality of your prints, Joshlyn."

Joshlyn was shocked. Of all the things she thought Ami wanted to talk about, this was not even in the realm of her thinking. Right now, she wasn't sure how to feel. By all rights, she should be ecstatic that someone liked her photos enough to want them in a series of books. She was exhilarated and terrified at the same time. What would this mean for her career, but more importantly, what would this mean for her solitude and the safe haven she'd built for herself?

"Joshlyn?"

"Um, yeah, I'm here."

"You can ask questions now if you want or if you just want to be left alone to think about it then I'll understand," Ami asked worriedly.

"Is this...I mean, who is this freelance writer?"

"Her name is Robin Masters." Ami smiled, waiting for Joshlyn's reaction. Robin Masters was a goddess among freelance writers. Her awe-inspiring articles had won more awards than any other freelance writer in her time. The kicker of it all was that Robin was in her early thirties, hardly a lifelong veteran by industry standards.

"*The* Robin Masters?"

"The one and only, Joshlyn. This is an incredible opportunity for you, which is the only reason I told her I'd talk to you about it. So, take some time and think about it and let me know your thoughts, okay?"

"Do you know what kind of books she wants to do?"

"She just mentioned that they were children's/young adult books about diversity in every form. She is supposed to send an email with all the details attached."

"All right. I'll give it some thought and let you know," Joshlyn hesitated. "That's all I can tell you right now, Ami."

"That's all I ask, Joshlyn. I've gotta run for now, but we'll touch base later."

"Have a good evening, and I'll let you know as soon as I make a decision."

"All right, honey. Tell that sexy woman of yours I said hello." Ami chuckled.

Joshlyn shook her head and smiled in spite of Ami's comment. "Good night!"

Joshlyn got up, put the phone back in its cradle, and stood leaning against the hall table.

"Wow! The Robin Masters wants me, Joshlyn Davis, to take pictures for her books!"

Joshlyn felt the excitement course through her

veins. The last thing she wanted to do right now was sit at home. No matter how terrified she was of putting herself out there for these books, she was thrilled nonetheless. She glanced at her watch and grinned. Joshlyn snagged her keys off the table and headed back out the door.

Kellen tossed the pencil down and growled. The software program she was working on needed an updated patch, but she was having a hard time coming up with one that would work with the current system yet give the owners the versatility they were wanting. She'd gone over the program with the company and tried to explain the program they had was outdated and needed to be completely overhauled, but to no avail. They were convinced that the program they purchased eight years prior should still be effective. At long last, Kellen threw up her hands and told them she'd give it a try, but there were no guarantees. For two hours now she'd been at it, with no luck in sight.

"Stupid ass programmers should have known better than to promise these people the type of longevity they did."

Kellen leaned back in her chair and ran her hands through her hair for the umpteenth time.

"Even you know better than that, Chigger."

Chigger was lying comfortably in front of her feet with his head on his paws. His ears perked, but that was about it.

"That's how it goes some days, buddy," Kellen continued, leaning down to rub the dog's head. "Tell the people what they want to hear whether it's the truth or not. Well, I'm done wasting my time with this. They'll either have to accept they need a new system or find someone else."

Kellen glanced at the clock and grinned. "C'mon boy, let's clean this mess up. It's almost time to call Joshlyn." She had gotten a later start on work this evening because she had stopped by Erin's for dinner. She always enjoyed her time and Erin was a fabulous cook. Conversation was easy as well. Kellen chuckled because it was a known fact that Erin could hold a conversation with a rock! Talking was definitely not a weak quality for her. It felt good to tell someone else how she was feeling about Joshlyn.

"So, what's her name?"

"What makes you think there is a her?"

"C'mon, Kellen, I'm no dummy. I can see the wheels turning inside that gorgeous head of yours."

Kellen grinned. She never could keep anything from her. "Joshlyn. We haven't known each other long, but it feels like forever. Does that even make sense?"

"It makes perfect sense. Have you two...you know?"

Kellen blushed. "We've been intimate, yes. I'm not saying this because of that, Erin. I felt this way before anything happened, which was quite recent I might add."

"I'm not saying you do, Kellen, I was just curious."

"She just feels like...like home. I don't even know how else to explain it."

"When it's meant to be, that's exactly how it should feel."

After Sunday's little chat, Kellen was afraid that Joshlyn would put some distance between them because she didn't ask any questions or push for any details. Much to Kellen's surprise, Joshlyn called her the next night and they talked for over an hour. When the conversation ended, Joshlyn asked her to call tonight. Kellen knew that Joshlyn was busy this week trying to get pictures done for her next session so phone calls would have to suffice. *God do I miss her, though!*

Kellen pushed her chair back and was starting to clean up her papers when the doorbell rang. She looked down at the papers in her hands and frowned.

"Dammit," she hissed, taking another peek at the clock.

She dropped the papers back on the desk and headed to the front door. The windows on each side of the door were marbled and obscured detail so she couldn't immediately see who was on the other side. She leaned her forehead against the door and looked out the peephole.

Kellen's frown immediately turned into a grin as she unlocked the door and opened it.

"What are you doing here?" Kellen said, standing in the doorway.

Joshlyn couldn't have responded if her life depended on it. She'd never seen Kellen in her work clothes and was damned glad she didn't have to work alongside her. Kellen's hair was down and flowing against her shoulders. It was mussed a little as if she'd been running her fingers through it. Her gorgeous blue eyes were adorned with small oval shaped glasses and her lips were full and moist. A tasteful vest in shades of khaki, light blue, and white was worn over a white oxford shirt, sleeves rolled partially up her forearms and unbuttoned almost to her cleavage where a delicate chain hung. Her shirt was tucked into navy slacks that hugged her hips like a new lover and her feet were bare. *Holy mother of God!*

"Hello, earth to Joshlyn," Kellen said, snapping her fingers in front of Joshlyn's face.

"Huh?"

Kellen laughed and repeated her earlier question. "What are you doing here?"

Joshlyn cleared her throat and shook the haze from her head. "Um, I thought I'd surprise you." Joshlyn stopped and raised her eyebrows. "But if you aren't happy to see me then I can leave."

Kellen grabbed Joshlyn's arm before she could even think of leaving. "Oh no, you're here now, don't think I'm going to let you go that easily."

Joshlyn smirked and followed Kellen inside.

Kellen turned and pulled Joshlyn into her arms. "I'm very glad you're here. I've missed you."

Kellen leaned close and kissed her. She wrapped her arms around Joshlyn and hugged her close. Ending the kiss, she smiled. "What an awesome surprise. You have no idea what a welcome sight you are."

Joshlyn returned the smile and gave her another quick kiss on the lips. "Yeah? Why's that?"

"This damned program I've been working on is giving me a headache. I've worked on it for over two hours and I just can't find the solution they want."

"Well, I'm sure if there was a solution you'd have found it, right?"

"I certainly tried, but I know that's not going to make them happy." Kellen sighed.

"On the whole, what does that mean for them?"

Kellen took Joshlyn's hand and led her to the couch. Taking a seat in the corner, she waited to continue until Joshlyn was comfortable.

"It means they are going to have to spend a little bit of money to upgrade their dinosaur of a program. I tried to explain that to them, but to no avail."

Joshlyn grabbed one of Kellen's feet and started to stroke the arch. "Then what else can you do?"

Kellen groaned and closed her eyes. "Notta."

Joshlyn chuckled and continued to massage her foot. "You're pretty tense."

"Mmmm."

Kellen let her foot be rubbed a little longer before finally cracking an eye. "Hey, you never said what brought you over here."

"Oh, that. Well, Ami called me earlier and had a bit of news to share with me."

"Yeah? Good news or bad news?"

"That is exactly what I was thinking. It turned out to be good news, I think."

"News you want to share or you were just too wound up to stay at home alone?"

"Both," Joshlyn decided.

"Then?"

"Seems Robin Masters contacted her today and wants me to work with her on a series of books."

Kellen's jaw dropped. She pulled her foot out of Joshlyn's hand and leaned forward. "Robin Masters as in renowned freelance writer…that Robin Masters?"

Joshlyn laughed and nodded her head. "Can you believe it?"

"Josh, that's fantastic! Are you going to do it?"

"I'm not sure yet. I'm going to think about it."

"Think about it? What's there to think about?" Kellen asked incredulously.

"I'm not sure I want that notoriety, Kellen. I mean, I have no idea what this will mean for me, but I do know with that famous of a writer there's no way I can maintain my anonymity."

Kellen knew Joshlyn was a private person, but had no idea it ran this deep. She sensed there were things Joshlyn didn't talk about, but never pushed.

"All right, I see your point. You *are* going to think about it though, right?"

"Of course. I'm not that stupid," Joshlyn replied, looking away.

Kellen slid across the couch so she was perched right next to Joshlyn. She tucked a finger under her chin and turned her head back around.

"Joshlyn, you are anything but stupid."

Kellen's gaze was lighting a fire low in her groin. As much as she wanted to explore this feeling, she didn't want Kellen to think she was ignoring her or trying to change the subject.

"I know," Joshlyn replied, quietly.

Kellen studied her for a moment longer before rubbing a hand on her leg.

"Have you eaten dinner yet?"

Joshlyn clasped her hand. "No, want to go grab something?"

"How about we hang here and I'll cook you dinner?"

"Oh, now that sounds like a deal I can't refuse."

"Great. Let me go get changed and I'll get busy."

❧ ❧ ❧ ❧

Kellen wiped her mouth, dropped the napkin on the plate, and pushed the plate away. She took a drink of tea and leaned back in her chair.

"This was fantastic, Kellen. You grill a mean

salmon," Joshlyn groaned, rubbing her stomach. "I am so full."

"Thank you, I'm glad you liked it."

"Are you done working for the night or do you need to get back to it?"

"I'm done. If I look at those papers anymore tonight I won't be responsible for my actions," Kellen grumbled. "Tomorrow I'll call and tell them there is no way to make an updated patch for a program that is non-existent at this point."

Joshlyn couldn't help but chuckle. She knew Kellen was serious, but her grumbling was cute. "Do you want to go watch some television for a little while then?"

Kellen smiled and stood. She pushed her chair in and held her hand up.

"Wait right here."

Joshlyn curiously watched her leave the room and come back with a small, lightweight throw blanket.

Kellen reached for Joshlyn's hand. "I've got a better idea. Come with me."

Joshlyn hopped up from her chair and followed Kellen out the back sliding glass door and across the deck. It was a gorgeous night. A slight breeze ruffled the leaves and the crickets were busy chirping away. The sky was clear and full of stars.

"When I was little, Granddaddy and I used to grab a blanket and curl up on the porch. We'd lay out watching the stars for hours," Kellen reminisced.

"I can remember some of the sleepovers I went on where we'd camp out in a tent in the yard. It may sound corny, but it was really a lot of fun."

Kellen led Joshlyn over to the hammock and stopped. "I don't think it sounds corny at all."

Kellen straddled the hammock and sat towards one end. "Here, you can sit facing me," she said, patting the other end.

Joshlyn drew her eyebrows up. "You want me to what?"

Kellen laughed and pulled her closer. "Here, just do what I'm doing and once you get seated you can lay your legs across my thighs. That way we can see each other and talk."

Precariously Joshlyn threw one leg across the hammock and sat down. "You sure this isn't going to tip over this way?"

"I'm positive, now come on."

Joshlyn brought her legs up and across Kellen's thighs and settled comfortably down into the hammock.

Kellen tossed the blanket across their laps and used a foot to set the hammock swaying.

"Granddaddy used to point out all the constellations. He loved teaching me all the little things he knew. He was such a wealth of information."

"He sounds like he was a wonderful man, someone you could really count on and turn to when you needed it the most."

"You know, I don't think there was anything I couldn't ask him about that he didn't know at least a little bit about it. I'd sit and listen to him until either he or I fell asleep." Kellen laughed. "More times than not we slept out on the porch."

Joshlyn smiled as Kellen recalled memories of her grandfather. It was very apparent that she held him in high regards. She wished she could recall fond memories and still feel good about them; instead, they left her feeling cold inside.

Kellen felt Joshlyn shiver and, mistaking it for her being cold, ran her hands up and down the legs lying across hers.

"Tell me more about your grandfather," Joshlyn asked.

"He had so many stories. Sometimes I wondered if they were all true. Stories about when he was a boy and all the trouble he'd get into."

"And you wonder if they were true? Take a look in the mirror. The apple doesn't fall far from the tree." Joshlyn laughed.

"Hey!" Kellen squeezed Joshlyn's thighs, making her sit upright.

"Just stating the obvious, sweetheart," she said, laying her arms across Kellen's shoulders.

"Anyhow…where was I?"

Joshlyn ran her fingers lightly through Kellen's hair, letting her thumbs graze gently across her ears.

"You were telling me what an ornery boy your grandfather was."

"Oh, right…um," Kellen was having a hard time concentrating with Joshlyn touching her. What she wanted to do was grab her and kiss her senseless.

"Ahuh, go on," Joshlyn chided.

"He, uh…" Kellen dropped her chin to her chest and gave up. She grabbed the front of Joshlyn's shirt and pulled her flush against her chest.

"What's wrong, Kel?" Joshlyn whispered.

"What's wrong is that you are driving me insane. The way you look at me, the way you touch me, the way you smell. I can't take it anymore."

"So what are you going to do about it?"

Kellen tilted her head and captured Joshlyn's lips. She started with slow, gentle nips before increasing the pressure, her tongue begging for entrance. Joshlyn emitted a groan of desire and wrapped her arms around Kellen.

Kellen lowered Joshlyn back against the hammock and brought a hand up between them. She placed her palm against a warm, supple breast and squeezed.

Joshlyn's heart accelerated rapidly as a rush of heat filled her groin. "Kellen."

Kellen locked eyes with Joshlyn. Carefully she brought one knee up beside Joshlyn's hip and shifted her body to bring the other one up. She'd no more than lifted her foot from the ground when the hammock tipped precariously.

Joshlyn felt the world spin as she landed with a heavy thud and felt a whoosh of air rush past her. She lay there for just a moment before realizing that Kellen was gasping for air.

Joshlyn scrambled off Kellen and grabbed her arm. "Oh my God, Kellen. Are you okay?"

Kellen tried to respond, but the air was slow to return to her lungs so she closed her eyes and tried to nod instead.

"All right, just relax and try to slow your breathing down."

"I'm okay," Kellen wheezed.

Joshlyn leaned down on an elbow and smoothed the hair back away from Kellen's face. Her breathing was slowly returning to normal.

"Doing okay?"

Kellen turned her head towards Joshlyn's voice and opened her eyes. "Definitely doing better than I was a few minutes ago. You okay?"

"Me?" Joshlyn chuckled. "Yeah, I had a soft landing, sweetheart."

Joshlyn rested her hand against Kellen's cheek and leaned closer. "I thought you said that thing wouldn't tip."

Kellen burst out laughing and then grabbed her chest. "Oh, don't make me laugh!"

Joshlyn brought her head the rest of the way down and captured Kellen's lips. Her hand moved down Kellen's neck and stopped over the rapidly beating pulse. Joshlyn kissed the smooth surface of Kellen's cheek before moving down to her chin. She placed small butterfly kisses across her jaw and nipped at the edge of her ear.

"You are so beautiful, Kellen," Joshlyn whispered before sliding down to taste the skin she couldn't seem to get enough of lately.

Kellen gasped and tilted her head back in submission. Her stomach tightened as Joshlyn's hands wandered lovingly over her body. She closed her eyes again, allowing herself a few minutes of peaceful bliss.

Joshlyn released the top three buttons on Kellen's lounge shirt and slipped a hand inside. The warm surface did nothing to dampen the flames of want coursing through her. She placed her lips against Kellen's chest and inhaled, losing herself in the heady scent. *Lordy but she smells good!*

"I want you..." Joshlyn rasped.

Kellen's stomach tightened. "What's stopping you, Joshlyn?"

Joshlyn glanced around the yard and raised her eyebrows. "Uh, we're outside. What about your neighbors?"

"We're fine," Kellen started and rushed on when Joshlyn was getting ready to object. "They can't see in the yard." She waited briefly. "Please?"

Joshlyn drew a deep breath. There was no way she could refuse Kellen and heaven knows she didn't want to either.

Kellen wrapped an arm around Joshlyn's neck and pulled her close, kissing her tentatively.

Joshlyn gave up the internal battle and resumed her exploring. She slid her hand down the front of Kellen's shirt to the waistband of her pants. Plucking at the edge, she slipped her fingers underneath and caressed the taut stomach that greeted her. Moving her hand between Kellen's legs, she stroked her slowly, letting the pressure build.

"Oh, Joshlyn," Kellen moaned.

"That's it, baby, let it go." Joshlyn moved faster against Kellen until she felt her shudder. She slowed the tempo, pulling a little more out of her.

Kellen blinked rapidly, trying to dislodge the tears blinding her. Words could not describe how Joshlyn made her feel.

Joshlyn kissed Kellen one last time before smiling down at her.

"I—" Kellen started.

Joshlyn placed a finger against her lips. "Shhhh, I know."

Chapter Fourteen

Kellen was late getting home from a meeting with a potentially new client. She tried in vain not to keep glancing at her watch and eventually the client had all his questions answered and agreed to give her a call after he made his decision. Driving as fast as she could without causing an accident, she made it home in record time. She grabbed her mail, rushed through the door, and tossed her keys on the table. Joshlyn had decided to go ahead and meet Robin Masters and get further details about what she wanted before she made her decision. Ami called with arrangements to meet for dinner and asked Joshlyn to bring Kellen along with her if she wanted. Taking another look at the clock, she had just enough time to shower and dress before Joshlyn would arrive. She filled Chigger's food and water dish and headed for the shower.

Kellen slipped into her clothes, sprayed a little cologne on, and headed back into the bathroom. She turned the blow dryer on low and ran her fingers through her hair. After a few minutes, she set it down.

"Dry enough."

Grabbing a tube of lip balm, she ran it over her lips before pocketing it. She flipped the light out and headed back to the kitchen.

"C'mere Chigger, wanna go outside?" Kellen asked, sliding the glass door open.

The pup's nails clicked on the tiled surface as he went outside.

Kellen picked up the mail and randomly went through it.

"Junk…junk…water bill…junk." She tossed the junk in the trash and the bills on the table. A nondescript white envelope sat in the middle of her mail with no return address. The closer she inspected it she realized it had no post mark on it either. She turned it over, slipped a finger under the flap, and opened it. Pulling the piece of paper out, she unfolded it and began to read.

"What the fuck…" Kellen turned the letter over in her hands and glanced at the back before turning it back around. The letter was simple and to the point in typed letters.

You best watch your back before
Someone sticks a knife in it.
You've been warned!

"Who the hell would send something like this?" Kellen asked nobody in particular. She placed the letter back in the envelope and tossed it on the table. Her teeth worked her lower lip as she wondered about the letter. There was only one person she could think of that would have any reason whatsoever to send her a fucked up letter with demands.

Before she could contemplate anything further, the doorbell rang. She hollered at Chigger and locked the sliding glass door. She snagged her jacket off the back of the couch and rushed to the front door.

Joshlyn stepped back to let Kellen out the door. Kellen grinned and kissed her before taking an arm and leading her to the car.

Kellen fastened her seatbelt and turned towards Joshlyn, waiting for her to get settled.

"So, are you excited?"

"More like nervous, to be honest. What if I really like her and this project is as perfect as it sounds?"

"Well, I guess you'll have some decisions to make then." Kellen hesitated. "Josh, what is it that stops you from wanting this so much? I mean, obviously I know something has happened in your past that has put you on the defensive, but so much so that you'd turn away an opportunity of a lifetime?"

"Don't you think I know that," Joshlyn snapped. She started the car and headed towards the restaurant. There was no way Kellen could understand how she felt or what she'd gone through and quite honestly she wasn't sure she was ready to share this part of her life yet. That said, there was no reason for her to bite Kellen's head off for not understanding and asking an innocent question. Was there any way she could make amends for the nasty response?

Kellen remained silent for the rest of the ride to the restaurant. The last thing she wanted to do was upset Joshlyn before going into this meeting, so she'd leave the ball in her court and see how she responded. This wasn't over by a long shot. Kellen learned long ago to shut her mouth after making the mistake of questioning her father over his involvement with some shady dealings. More often than not, she had been the recipient of his harsh tongue. His drinking left him uninhibited and he said exactly what was on his mind. The verbal stuff she eventually learned to tune out, but the physical violence scared her into submission. Her father was a mean son of a bitch and it only took one lesson for her to learn that as long as she was under his roof she would not cross him. The beating she received landed her in the hospital for almost a week. Nobody knew her father had beat her. She told everyone that she was walking home from school and was jumped. At sixteen, they took Kellen at her word. Kellen didn't know if she'd ever share this bit of information with another soul again. The one time she had, it was used against her.

She glanced out the window and watched the trees and flowers go by. Lots of people were out walking in the early evening. *I hate this silence! Why didn't I just keep my mouth shut?*

Joshlyn pulled into a parking spot and before Kellen could get out of the car, she grabbed her hand.

"Kellen, I'm really sorry for being such a bitch. You didn't deserve that."

Kellen squeezed her hand. "It's okay. We can talk about it later, but for now let's go meet Ms. Masters and see if she's worth all the hype, what do you say?"

Joshlyn smiled at her reprieve, temporary as it may be. "All right, that sounds good."

The restaurant was busy, but Ami was standing right up front waiting for them. They made their way through the bustling crowd and stopped beside her.

Ami gave Joshlyn a hug. "She'll be along shortly. We're going to go ahead and get a drink while waiting. She said she had a business call she had to take, but wouldn't be too long."

Joshlyn nodded. "Okay."

Ami leaned around Joshlyn and shook Kellen's hand. "It's good to see you again, Kellen. How've you been?"

"Hey, Ami, been good, thank you. How about

yourself?"

The hostess arrived and picked up some menus. "If you ladies will follow me, I'll show you to your seats."

"Same ole, same ole, you know how it goes."

Kellen honestly didn't know considering every day was different for her, but agreed anyhow.

"Here you ladies go. Your waitress tonight will be Lisa. Can I get you something to drink while you're waiting?"

After ordering their drinks, Ami leaned forward and regarded Joshlyn. "So, any idea which way you are thinking about going on this?"

"I really don't know, Ami. I mean, the offer is amazing, there's no doubting that, but I need to hear all the details before I decide."

"It's an opportunity that only comes along once in a blue moon, so be sure that whatever you decide is really what you want, Joshlyn."

Joshlyn fiddled with the napkin on her lap. She got it already that this was a big deal. How could she tell Ami to back off and let her make her own decision without her constantly reminding her of what she'd potentially be throwing away if she decided not to do it?

Kellen cleared her throat. "Ami, I think Joshlyn is more than prepared to listen to the details and then make a good sound decision based on what she's heard."

Ami glanced from Joshlyn to Kellen and then back to Joshlyn. "Well, yes, of course. I didn't mean to infer that you weren't capable. I just…well, I'm only looking out for you. You know how much I value the work you do for my company. I just want what's best, that's all."

Joshlyn reached over and clasped Ami's hand. "I know you do and I appreciate it. So, tell me about Robin Masters. What should I expect?"

"I think you are going to be pleasantly surprised with her. I expected some super bitch based on the recognition she is receiving, but she's really very sweet and down to earth."

Joshlyn was about to ask another question when the waitress arrived with their drinks.

"Are you ladies ready to order yet?"

"We are waiting for one more in our party, but then we'll be ready," Ami answered.

The waitress glanced around the table and briefly stopped when her eyes landed on Kellen. She tipped her head slightly and then continued on. "Very well. My name's Lisa. I'll keep an eye out for the other member of your party. If you should need anything until then, please don't hesitate to ask."

"Thank you, Lisa," Joshlyn replied with a touch of sarcasm.

The waitress placed her pen and tablet in her smock and walked away. Ami lasted all of five seconds before she burst out laughing. Joshlyn glanced first at Ami and then at Kellen, who was smiling shyly.

"What?" Joshlyn huffed.

Ami wiped a tear from her eye. "Nothing, honey."

Kellen leaned towards Joshlyn and whispered, "You couldn't have claimed ownership any better than if you'd stood up and pissed on me."

"What the hell are you talking about, Kel?"

"Joshlyn, your eyes couldn't be any greener if you tried." Ami giggled.

Joshlyn sat motionless, her eyes wide with shock. Suddenly she felt the urge to bolt from the room, Robin Masters and her wonderful offer be damned. Her heart felt like it was going to beat right out of her chest.

"Um, excuse me for a moment, will you," Joshlyn asked, but didn't wait for a response. She hopped up from her chair and made her way to the ladies room.

Pushing the door open, Joshlyn almost knocked a petite redhead over in the process.

"Oh, I'm sorry," Joshlyn stammered and sidestepped the woman.

"My mistake," the redhead responded. "I'm always late and never watching where I'm going. Pardon me, lass."

Joshlyn smiled politely and proceeded to an open stall. Closing the door, she sagged against the wall and willed her legs to support her a little longer. *Dammit!* Joshlyn took several deep breaths and slowly calmed. She realized now that Ami's comment was completely harmless, but still she couldn't keep herself from reacting. There was no way she could explain that her response had nothing to do with the teasing gesture, but the comment itself that hit too close to home. *What must Ami and Kellen be thinking? They are probably thinking you've lost your fucking mind!* Joshlyn knew she couldn't hide out in the restroom the remainder of the night. How rude would that be? Releasing the catch on the door, Joshlyn walked over to the bank of mirrors and sinks. She dampened a paper towel and patted at her throat and forehead then leaned closer and blinked several times.

Joshlyn took one last breath and headed back to the table.

Ami stared at Kellen after Joshlyn's quick departure. "What the hell just happened?"

"I have absolutely no idea, Ami. Maybe she's just worked up about this possible new project. I know she doesn't want to make the wrong decision."

"Should I go talk to her or let her come back on her own?"

Kellen thought about it for a minute before responding. "Honestly, I'd let her come back on her own. As quick as she left I think she wanted some time alone to collect herself."

"I hope she doesn't take too long because that's Robin Masters coming this way right now," Ami pointed out.

Kellen watched the compact woman approach. For such a tiny thing, she sure moved fast. Her bobbed red hair was pushed back behind both ears and her smile was very engaging. Kellen immediately liked her.

As the woman approached the table, she held out her hand to Ami. "I'm so sorry I'm late, please forgive me. Any other time I'd have told the bloke to stuff a sock in it, but alas he is my source of income this month."

And charming as well, Kellen surmised.

Ami laughed and stood to greet the newcomer. "Hello, Ms. Masters, it's good to see you this evening."

"Oh please, it's Robin. No sense in formalities here." She grinned.

"Very well; Robin this is—,"

"Joshlyn, I presume," Robin interrupted, leaning

over to shake her hand.

"Uh, no. I'm Kellen, a friend of Joshlyn's," Kellen responded shaking the hand in front of her.

"Ah, forgive me, Kellen. It is so nice to meet you."

Kellen smiled. "Likewise. I've heard wonderful things about your work."

Ami placed a hand on Robin's shoulder and gestured to her right. "This is the photographer you want to meet. Robin, I'd like to introduce you to Joshlyn Davis. Joshlyn, this is Robin Masters."

Joshlyn stopped short of the table, feeling slightly embarrassed. As she walked up, she knew Robin would recognize her from their near collision.

Robin held out a hand. "We meet again, Ms. Joshlyn Davis."

Joshlyn clasped Robin's hand and smiled. "It's very nice to meet you, Ms. Masters."

"Ah, it's Robin, please. Shall we sit down and eat and hammer out some of the details? I'm famished!"

They all agreed, sat down, and opened their menus.

Joshlyn felt immediately at ease around Robin. Her personality was not what she had expected. The word 'diva' came to mind, but Robin acted as if she was no different from the person at the next table; it was very refreshing. Joshlyn glanced up from her menu and found Kellen peeking over her menu at her. She cracked a small grin when Kellen winked at her and went back to studying her menu. Gradually she felt her shoulders relax and when the waitress came back around, they all ordered.

"So," Robin started, slicing through a piece of chicken with her knife. She speared the piece of food and pointed at Joshlyn with the fork. "It's you I want, Joshlyn. I don't mind groveling if I have to. I've seen your work and it's what I want." She popped the bite in her mouth and chewed.

"I'm very flattered, Robin, but I really need to know what you're wanting before I can agree to anything."

Robin took a sip of water and set her glass down. "It's really very simple. I'm looking for unification through diversity. I want to show diverse situations in every facet and at the end we'll show how they all connect to make us all the same."

"Simple, huh?" Joshlyn gulped. "And do you have a timeline for completion of this project?"

"Ah, see this is where it gets easy. The sooner the better, yes, but I don't want to rush you, Joshlyn. I know that sometimes it takes the right moment to get the perfect shot so I'm not rushing you on this. When you feel you have the pictures for what we need, then it'll be done. Until then, you're the boss."

Joshlyn stared, completely dumbfounded.

"That's it? You're leaving it all up to me?"

Robin chuckled. "Not all of it, but it's not my words that will make the difference with this, Joshlyn, it's your pictures. You know what they say, don't you? A picture is worth a thousand words."

Joshlyn cleared her throat and set her fork down. "When do you need to know my decision?"

"I know this was sudden so I don't want to push, but do you think you could make a decision within the next week? The sooner I can let my people know the quicker they can get moving on things." Robin pulled a cardholder out of her front pocket and removed a business card. "All the numbers you can reach me at plus my email address are on that card. If you want, you can go to the website listed and see some of the other stuff I've done."

Joshlyn slipped the card in her pocket. "I've seen quite a bit of your work, actually. I was surprised when Ami told me you were interested in *my* work."

"Well, you shouldn't be, lass. Those are some mighty fine prints you've taken, if I do say so myself."

Kellen took pity on the profusely blushing Joshlyn and piped into the conversation. "Where do you get your ideas, Robin?"

Mischievous brown eyes twinkled at Kellen. "The question isn't where my ideas come from, it's where *don't* they come from."

Kellen laughed. "I see your point."

"Ladies, let me clear some of these plates out of your way. Did you save room for dessert this evening?" the waitress asked.

"I'm good, but I could use a cup of coffee," Ami responded.

"Anyone else?"

Kellen, Joshlyn, and Robin agreed on coffee as well.

"So, Kellen, I've been sitting here wondering where it is that I've seen you before and it finally clicked," Robin said, snapping her fingers.

Kellen's brows furrowed. "Yeah? Where's that?"

"You're one of those racecar drivers they featured the other night. Don't remember which channel it was, but it was a national broadcast program and they were talking about some new and upcoming drivers on the amateur circuit."

Joshlyn's spine stiffened. She reached for the creamer and dropped a couple dollops into her cup.

"Really?" Kellen sat up a little straighter.

"Yep. They showed some highlights from that race you did last weekend. That was pretty amazing! They also showed some of your local interview. I caught a quick glimpse of Joshlyn before they zoomed in on you."

Kellen was so intent on what Robin had to say that she missed Joshlyn's reaction to the last statement. Her face completely drained of color and she felt like her dinner was about to reappear. She took deep breaths, trying to calm the storm running loose in her stomach.

"That's incredible. I had no idea it extended beyond local media. Did you know that Ami's brother was a driver as well?" Kellen asked.

"No. It looks like a bloody good time though. So, between us, how awesome is it to go that fast?" Robin rubbed her hands together.

Kellen and Ami both laughed. "Nothing compares!" Kellen assured.

They visited a little longer until Robin finally said she needed to run because she had an early meeting in the morning.

Robin rested a hand on Joshlyn's shoulder. "Joshlyn, it was really great to meet you. I look forward to hearing from you." She patted her shoulder and then extended a hand towards Kellen.

Kellen shook her hand. "It was nice to meet you."

"You ladies keep in touch." Robin turned towards Joshlyn one last time. "I know we can make this work. Give me a call, okay?"

Joshlyn gave a slight smile and nodded. "Okay."

"Girls, I will see you later. Dinner was wonderful. We should do this more often," Ami remarked. She leaned in to give Joshlyn a hug goodbye and waved to Kellen.

Kellen placed a hand at the small of Joshlyn's back and led her out to the car. Joshlyn had grown increasingly quiet at the end of their visit with Robin. She chalked it up to nerves and the upcoming decisions she knew Joshlyn had to make. The longer they rode in the car, though, the more Kellen worried.

Kellen reached across the console and laced her fingers with Joshlyn's. "You okay?"

"I'm fine," Joshlyn replied without taking her eyes off the road.

"Tired?"

"A little."

Conversation was not easily forthcoming and Kellen wasn't sure she wanted to force it if Joshlyn wasn't in the mood. Maybe she'd be better off just saying goodnight and heading home to Chigger.

Joshlyn pulled the car into her drive, turned it off, and sat there for a moment. She leaned her head against the steering wheel and took a deep breath.

Kellen sat pensively, chewing on her lower lip. She had no idea what was going through Joshlyn's mind, but sensed it was something big.

Joshlyn sat up. "Why don't you come in, Kellen. We need to talk."

Chapter Fifteen

Kellen followed Joshlyn into the house and waited while she closed the door, set her things on the table, and turned back around.

"Go ahead and have a seat," Joshlyn indicated with a sweep of her hand at the couch. She had hoped this day would never come, but deep down knew it would. It was now or never because she doubted she would have the courage later.

Kellen sat precariously on the edge of the couch, waiting for Joshlyn to tell her what was going on.

"Would you like something to drink?"

Kellen shook her head. "No, thank you. Can you just tell me what's going on, Joshlyn?"

Joshlyn stared into Kellen's eyes. The worry was clearly evident and Joshlyn hated herself for making Kellen feel the way she was, but it couldn't be avoided. She took a deep breath and turned her back on Kellen. There was no way she could tell her what she needed to say while looking her in the face.

"I've been doing a lot of thinking and I think we need to cool things off."

When there was no response from Kellen, Joshlyn took a quick glance over her shoulder. Her chest ached at the forlorn look on Kellen's face. She rushed ahead, determined to say what needed to be said. "I'm not saying I don't want to see you at all, Kellen, I'd like to remain friends."

Kellen felt her heart sink. Of all the things she expected Joshlyn to say, this wasn't it. She opened her mouth to speak, but couldn't find the words. Instead, she sat dumbfounded, waiting for the other shoe to drop. Joshlyn stood stock still with her back still turned.

Kellen was so stunned she couldn't even blink. Her mind was having a hard time comprehending what Joshlyn was saying.

"Uh, wait a minute, back up."

Joshlyn turned fully around to face Kellen now.

"Can you please sit down so we can talk about this?" Kellen asked, patting the surface next to her.

Joshlyn shook her head. "I'd rather stand and say what I've got to say."

Kellen stood and moved in front of Joshlyn. "What about me? What about what I have to say, Joshlyn?"

"This isn't about you, Kellen."

"Excuse me? How could this not be about me when I'm the one you're breaking up with?" Kellen exclaimed, growing angrier by the minute.

"I don't expect you to understand."

"Well, that's a damned good thing because I can assure you that I don't understand." Kellen started pacing in back and forth in front of Joshlyn.

"Kel, please—"

"Don't," Kellen rasped. It was hard enough listening without her using the shortened version of her name.

"Just tell me why, Joshlyn," Kellen begged, stopping in front of her.

Joshlyn's spine stiffened as she crossed her arms across her chest. Her defensive posture spoke volumes.

"I have my reasons, Kellen, and that's all you need to know."

Kellen took a step closer and grasped Joshlyn's upper arms in her hands.

"Fuck reasons, Joshlyn. The least you can do is give me the courtesy of an explanation. Don't I at least deserve that?"

Joshlyn jerked her arms away from Kellen's hands. She felt the heat rise in her neck and up into her cheeks. This isn't how she wanted this to happen, but if Kellen wanted a fight, she'd get one. *Damn, why couldn't she just leave it alone!*

"You don't have a Goddamned clue about anything, Kellen. You think you're so high and mighty, but let me just tell you a little something, you aren't, so climb down off that ladder and get your head out of the clouds."

"What? Who the hell do you think you are?" Kellen exclaimed.

"You wanted answers, well, I'll give them to you because you certainly can't figure them out for yourself." Joshlyn was on a roll and as much as it hurt to do this, she knew she couldn't stop now. *Please forgive me, baby. I didn't want to hurt you like this.*

Kellen fumed. This was going from bad to worse in a matter of seconds. Her breathing was coming in short gasps now.

Joshlyn leaned closer to Kellen. "Listen to me very closely, Kellen Reynolds. You will never be more than a drunk's little grease monkey!"

Joshlyn couldn't have pushed her point any further home than if she'd stuck it on the end of a knife and drove it into Kellen's chest. Tears immediately sprang to Kellen's eyes as she struggled to catch her breath.

Joshlyn turned and walked to the door; grasping the handle, she pulled it open.

"Now, get out." *God, just go...please don't make me hurt you anymore.*

Kellen didn't know how she managed, but she pulled her keys out of her pocket and moved towards the door. She stopped in front of Joshlyn as the tears fell from her eyes.

"Why, Joshlyn?" Kellen asked, but she really didn't expect an answer. She dropped her head and stepped outside. The door closed behind her and as the lock clicked, she felt the last push of the knife enter her chest.

❧ ❧ ❧ ❧

As soon as the door closed, Joshlyn dropped her head against it. *Shit, shit, shit!* She'd driven tonight and now Kellen was on the other side of the door with no way home. She glanced out the peephole and could see Kellen standing in the middle of the sidewalk. Squaring her shoulders, she opened the door.

"Kellen."

Kellen turned just enough to acknowledge her.

"Do you want me to call you a cab?"

Kellen hadn't even thought that far ahead. She glanced down at the useless keys in her hand and tried to take a deep breath. Right now, she was trying to wrap her head around all that just happened. Joshlyn broke up with her, insulted her, and now wanted to push one last button by trying to be nice.

"Don't bother, I can find my own way home," Kellen responded and turned her back on the one person she really thought she could trust.

"Fine." *She wants to be stubborn then she can find her own way home. Damn, she was infuriating! Stubborn, infuriating and ugh…sexy as hell!*

Joshlyn slammed the door, relocked it, and dropped to the floor. She buried her face in her hands. "Oh my God, what have I done?"

She let the tears fall. She cried for all the things she couldn't control and even more for the things she could, but was too terrified to even know where to begin. She wept until she was out of tears and sat hiccupping.

How would she ever be able to face Ami? Surely Emerson would talk to her and she'd find out soon enough about the break up. Maybe it was time to move on. A change of scenery wouldn't be so bad. *Keep kidding yourself, Joshlyn. You know the last thing you want to do is move again.*

"Fuck," she spat, slamming a fist to the floor. Slowly Joshlyn got her feet under her and pulled herself up from the floor. She made sure the door was locked and turned the front light out. Heading down the hall to the bedroom, she stopped in her office to shut down the computer for the night. As she leaned down, her eye caught the stack of pictures still sitting on her desk. She straightened back up and pulled them towards her. They were duplicates of the ones she'd given to Kellen. Right on top was the one of Kellen smiling right at the camera.

Joshlyn ran a hand over the image in front of her. "I hope one day you'll forgive me," she whispered.

She set the pictures back on the desk, shut the computer down, and turned the light out. Walking the last few steps to her bedroom, Joshlyn unbuttoned her shirt and pulled it off. She stripped out of the rest of her clothes and let them drop in a pile on the floor. After slipping into a t-shirt, she sat on the bed, pulled open the drawer of her nightstand, and took the wooden box into her hands.

"This is the last time I get involved with anyone. I can't take this kind of pain again," Joshlyn said quietly. She opened the box like she had so many other nights, but this time she moved the objects around and pulled the lone article from underneath the stack of papers. She didn't need to read the article that essentially ruined her life. She knew it word for word.

Dropping the article back into the box, she closed the lid. She took a deep breath and, screaming, she flung the box across the room. It splintered the instant it hit the wall, sending pieces of wood across the floor.

Joshlyn's insides were in turmoil. Part of her felt a little bit of joy at flinging the offending box away from her and the other part felt like it was going to throw up. If only life could be so easy.

She turned out the light and scooted down under the covers. Sleep would be a long time in coming. Joshlyn didn't know if she would ever forget the look on Kellen's face. The last comment Joshlyn made was flat nasty, but she wanted Kellen to run and never look back. It would be easier for the both of them.

❧ ❧ ❧ ❧

Kellen paid the cab driver and hurried up the walk. As she fit the key in the lock, she could hear Chigger barking. She moved through the door and on autopilot, she went through the kitchen and let the dog outside. She stood in the kitchen, not really knowing what to do. Of all the things that could have happened tonight, she never expected Joshlyn to hurt her the way she did. She could forgive Joshlyn of almost anything, but wasn't sure she'd ever forget the last comment. Hell, even the grease monkey part didn't bother her, but linking her with the man she despised hurt the most.

Kellen let the pup back in and closed the door. She wandered back into the living room and spotted the newly hung pictures on her wall. She stepped over to one and ran a finger over the smile on her face. It was meant for the person on the other side of the camera. *Joshlyn.* That day was one of the best days she could ever recall. Kellen felt the pressure of anger building inside her again. How could Joshlyn throw what they had away so easily? Furthermore, why would she want to throw it away? Kellen was having a hard time making sense of something that shouldn't be so unfamiliar to her. After all, being left behind was nothing new. Dejected, Kellen's shoulders slumped.

Her mother left, her grandfather left, and now Joshlyn was gone.

Kellen dropped down on the couch and curled into a ball. Once the tears started flowing, Kellen couldn't stop them. She cried harder than she could ever remember crying. Her soul felt shattered in tiny pieces. She ached in places she didn't know could ache.

At some point Chigger hopped up on the couch and curled up beside her. Eventually her tears waned and dried. She wasn't sure how long she lay on the couch and honestly didn't care. She really didn't care about anything at this point.

The dog whined and nudged his way under her

arm.

Kellen sniffed. "Except you; I do care about you, you little faker." She scratched his neck and ran her hand over his head. "I knew you could jump up here."

Chigger turned over on his back, waiting for Kellen to rub his belly.

"What am I going to do, boy?" she whispered against the pup's head. She closed her eyes, praying that when she woke up this would all be a dream, a very bad dream.

Chapter Sixteen

Joshlyn lay in bed, ignoring everything going on around her. The phone rang several times, but she let the machine answer it. She had no motivation whatsoever. The world could crumble around her and it would be an insignificant drop in the bucket as far as she was concerned. Sighing, Joshlyn rolled to her back. The only thing she wanted to do was try to forget that last night ever happened. Breaking up with Kellen was the second hardest thing she ever had to do. Sweet, beautiful, loving Kellen. Tears gathered in her eyes and dropped silently onto the pillow below her head.

"Laying here in bed all day isn't going to make getting over Kellen any easier," Joshlyn mumbled. "Might as well get up and do something productive."

Tossing the covers aside, Joshlyn sat up and swung her legs over the side of the bed. She traipsed to the bathroom and brushed her teeth. After spitting the toothpaste out and rinsing her mouth, she set the cup down and glanced in the mirror. The dark circles under her eyes exemplified exactly how she felt. *Miserable.* She dripped some eye drops into her tired and scratchy eyes.

Joshlyn pulled some cotton lounge pants on and headed to the kitchen to make a pot of coffee. She passed the answering machine along the way and erased the messages without even listening to them. While the coffee perked, she leaned against the counter, staring off into nothingness. Before Kellen came into the picture, the mundane tasks in her everyday life were easy to deal with. She didn't have to answer to anybody and her actions only affected herself. Now everything had changed. No matter how she tried to explain it, she was sure Kellen wouldn't have understood. Rather than take a chance, Joshlyn knew she had to end it. Whether forgiveness was in her future, she couldn't stand the thought of it affecting Kellen in any way.

A knock on the front door drew her attention. She walked to the door and peered out the peephole. Joshlyn dropped her chin to her chest and sighed. This was not who she wanted to face. Maybe she could just not answer the door and they'd go away.

"Joshlyn, I know you're in there so you might as well open up," Ami hollered through the door.

Damn! Go away...please just go away.

Ami banged on the door a little harder. "Your car is in the driveway and you're not answering the phone. Come on, Joshlyn. Open the door and talk to me. Please?"

Joshlyn blew a breath out, unlocked the door, and opened it. "What do you want, Ami?"

"Honey, you're as predictable as they come," Ami commented as she stepped into the living room.

Joshlyn gave a harsh laugh. "Predictable, huh? I'm sure you won't think that for long."

"What's going on?" Ami asked, putting a hand on Joshlyn's arm.

"Listen, if we're going to talk I need coffee. Want some?"

"Sure."

Joshlyn led Ami into the kitchen and poured

them both a cup of coffee. Setting them on the table, she indicated that Ami should have a seat.

Ami sipped her coffee in silence, giving Joshlyn the time she needed to talk.

Joshlyn was sure that Ami wouldn't let the subject go so the sooner she said something the sooner they could move on. Problem was, she didn't even know where to start.

"Ami, I know you want some answers but I honestly don't know where to begin."

"I don't want to pry, but I've sensed for a while that you needed to talk."

When Joshlyn continued to hesitate, Ami continued. "You know that whatever you tell me will stay between us. You can trust me, Joshlyn."

Joshlyn felt tears threatening and blinked her eyes against it. She was so tired of always fighting the battle on her own. Being strong this time around was a lot harder than what she imagined. Slowly the tears she tried to hold back coursed down her cheeks.

"Joshlyn," Ami began. She couldn't sit still any longer as her friend sat crying so she pulled her chair close to Joshlyn and wrapped her arms around her. "Ssshhh, go ahead and cry, sweetie."

Joshlyn cried so hard her body shook with the force. The despair she felt tore through her, leaving a gaping hole where her heart should be.

Ami became very concerned with the intensity of Joshlyn's emotions. Whatever happened was major. Eventually Joshlyn's sobs subsided enough for her to talk.

"I'm sorry," Joshlyn sniffled.

"Don't be sorry, hon. You obviously needed the release and I'm glad you felt comfortable enough to do it in front of me.”

"I don't know what I'm going to do, Ami."

"About what, Joshlyn?"

Joshlyn brought her head up and looked right into Ami's eyes. "Kellen has stolen my heart and in return I broke hers."

Ami tried to stifle a gasp, but she never imagined this would be what Joshlyn had to say. "I just saw you girls last night. What's happened between then and now?"

Joshlyn struggled because right now she wanted to blurt everything out. How she'd not only broke things off, but hurt Kellen in the worst possible way. However, she also felt that if she were going to finally be honest with Ami that she needed to start from the beginning.

"Ami, before we talk about that there's something you need to know."

Ami sat up in her chair and observed Joshlyn for a moment. Her nervous hands were fidgeting with her coffee cup and her eyes were everywhere but where they should be.

"How about we get another cup of coffee and you can tell me everything you want to share?"

"Okay."

Ami took Joshlyn's cup as well and refilled them both. She sat back down and waited attentively.

"What I'm getting ready to tell you I've never told another soul. I… it's important that I have your word that you won't share this with anyone."

"Joshlyn, you know you have my word."

"Nobody, Ami, and that includes Kellen."

"All right," Ami said, nodding.

Joshlyn knew she couldn't disclose everything,

but there was still a lot she could say. Deep down she trusted Ami and getting a load off her chest was just what she needed.

"Three years ago my life changed. I never expected it and certainly didn't welcome it. I'm not the same person I was at that time, Ami. Some things happened that forced me to relocate, change my name, and begin a new career. I hope you will understand that I don't want to delve into some of the details, but they were life threatening."

Ami sat in shock. The idea that this dear woman endured so much already was heartbreaking at the least. She felt afraid for Joshlyn, knowing that sharing this type of information would stir up past memories.

Joshlyn continued after taking a sip of her coffee. "With that in mind you can imagine my surprise when Robin said she saw us on the television the other night."

"Wait, Joshlyn, you knew Kellen was interviewed and on the local news the other night. Why is what Robin said any different?"

"Yes, I knew about that, but did you hear what Robin said? She saw the broadcast on a national show…national, Ami."

"Ok, so what does that have to do with you?"

"She said she saw a glimpse of me before they zoomed in on Kellen. If those people saw that then Kellen would be in danger, not to mention the fact that they saw me."

Ami didn't even know how to respond. This was definitely more information than she knew what to do with.

Joshlyn grabbed Ami's hand. "Do you see why I couldn't let that happen? I wouldn't be able to live with myself if anything happened to Kellen because of me."

"Joshlyn, what exactly did you do?"

"I brought Kellen back here last night and told her we needed to talk. I broke up with her."

"Oh, sweetie."

"It was horrible, Ami. She wanted an explanation and I couldn't give it to her."

"Why didn't you just tell her what you told me?"

"Because I know her well enough to know she wouldn't let things end. She'd make excuses and say we could work it out. I can't...no, I *won't* let anyone hurt her." Joshlyn ducked her head and said quietly, "It would kill me."

"If you knew she wouldn't give up, what did you say to make sure things ended, Joshlyn?"

"She will never forgive me." Joshlyn relayed the last part of the conversation she'd had with Kellen and then threw her hands up in defeat. "You know how she feels about her father."

Ami nodded, but did not comment.

"Then to make matters worse, I drove last night so when she stormed out she didn't have a car to get home. I offered to call a cab, but she told me not to bother."

"So, you haven't talked to her or heard from her since she left?"

Joshlyn chewed on the side of her lip and shook her head.

"Do you want me to go by and check on her?"

Joshlyn perked up just a little, but still seemed a little pensive.

"I promise not to say anything to her, but I do want to know that she got home okay."

"Okay and could you tell her…" Joshlyn stopped. *Tell her what? Tell her what an idiot I am and does she think she can ever forgive me? Give it up, Joshlyn, and let her go.*

Ami waited for Joshlyn to finish her sentence. "Nothing. Will you let me know if she's okay, Ami?"

"I will, but you'll have to answer your damn phone in order to find out."

Joshlyn smiled. "I'm not going anywhere. I promise I'll answer."

"All right then, hang in there, kiddo, and I'll call you later."

Joshlyn stood and followed Ami to the front door. "Thank you, Ami. You really are a good friend."

"Any time, Joshlyn; just remember I'm here if you need to talk."

❧ ❧ ❧ ❧

Ami approached Kellen's front door to knock, but stopped abruptly. The door was slightly ajar and Kellen's keys were dangling from the lock. She removed the keys and pushed the door open a little farther. She poked her head just inside the open door and felt immediately relieved. Not knowing for sure what to expect, the sight of Kellen curled up on the couch asleep and Chigger standing guard was more than welcomed.

"Poor thing," Ami whispered to herself. As she got closer, she could see twin trails of dried tears down Kellen's cheeks. She crouched down beside the couch and scratched Chigger under the chin.

Ami studied Kellen for a moment before placing a hand on her shoulder. She rubbed lightly, trying to rouse the sleeping woman. "Kellen, sweetie." When that failed to get a reaction, Ami gave her arm a little shake. "Kellen, come on, open your eyes for me."

Kellen could feel someone shaking her and talking to her, but she felt so tired and just wanted to sleep. It took all her strength to finally crack open an eye.

"What," Kellen rasped. Clearing her throat, she tried again. "What are you doing here?"

"You left your front door ajar and the keys hanging out of the lock." Ami dropped the keys on the coffee table and turned back to look at Kellen. "You okay?"

Kellen sat up on the couch and rubbed her tired eyes. They felt gritty and dry. She dropped her hands in her lap and regarded Ami. Assuming Ami had already talked to Joshlyn then she knew everything that transpired the previous night.

"Okay as compared to what?"

Kellen stood and walked to the kitchen. She opened the back door and let Chigger outside. Filling the coffee pot with water and dropping some grounds into the basket, she pushed the start button and rested her hands on the counter.

Ami pulled out a chair and sat down. She'd wait for Kellen to turn around before saying anything else.

Kellen closed her eyes and took some calming breaths. After losing Kerri she didn't think she'd ever feel this kind of pain again, but boy was she sadly mistaken. Kellen was never one to turn her back on a chance at love and given the opportunity to do it over, she wouldn't do anything different with Joshlyn than she'd already done. She just wished it didn't hurt so much. All the times she'd loved and lost should make letting go easier than this.

Kellen poured two cups of coffee and sat with Ami at the table. She took a sip before looking at Ami.

"Already talk to Joshlyn this morning?"

Ami nodded her head. "I just came from there."

Kellen made a noncommittal hum and took another drink of coffee.

"Kellen, if it's any consolation at all, she's just as torn up about this as you are."

Kellen felt half-pissed that Ami would come in here and defend Joshlyn's actions. "You've got to be kidding me, Ami. She's the one that ended this, not me."

"It doesn't make it any easier, Kellen."

"Don't." Kellen stopped her with a hand. "Don't sit there and try and make me feel sorry for her. She tore my heart out and then stomped all over it."

"Kellen, I'm not going to make excuses for her, but if you care about her at all please give her some time."

"Time for what? To inflict more damage than she's already done? No, thank you."

Kellen was getting very agitated. She didn't want Ami sitting in her kitchen defending Joshlyn and making her feel sorry for something she had no control over. She walked over to the sliding glass door and let Chigger back in. Leaning against the open door, she let the morning breeze waft over her. The hammock swayed lightly and the leaves rustled. She just wanted the pain to go away so she could get back to the life she was most comfortable with.

Ami walked up behind Kellen and looped an arm around her waist. "Do you care about her, Kellen?"

"What kind of fucking question is that? You

know I do," Kellen stated, staring into the yard.

"Then give her some time and try and talk to her again. That's all I'm asking."

Kellen turned slightly. "Is there something you aren't telling me, Ami? Because there is definitely something standing in the way."

"I..." Ami hedged. She didn't want to lie to Kellen, but she made a promise to Joshlyn. "What I do know is that Joshlyn cares about you, too."

Kellen studied Ami for a moment then turned back to watch a small sparrow play in the birdbath.

"I'm gonna go, but if you need anything, please call, okay?"

"'kay."

Ami gave Kellen's back a rub and then turned to leave.

Kellen stood still until she heard the distinct click of the front door. She tucked her head to her chest and willed the ache in her throat from unshed tears to dissipate. What did Ami know that she wasn't saying? And why would Kellen subject herself to another round of heartache if she didn't have to? None of it made sense.

Kellen closed the door and locked it. She placed the coffee cups in the sink and turned the coffee pot off.

"Come on, Chigger. I think you and I need to get out. Let's go for a walk, boy."

Chapter Seventeen

Kellen pulled into the garage and grabbed her things. She was very thankful that it was finally Friday. This week's race was tonight instead of the usual Saturday evening. The last two days were hell. She'd made sure that she had enough to keep her busy from the time she got up until late in the evening when she dragged herself home and fell into bed. As long as she didn't have to think about anything but work, then she was fine. The rare moments she allowed herself to think of Joshlyn were few and far between. After Ami left the other day, Kellen took Chigger on a long walk. They ended up at the off leash park and she let Chigger loose to run. She found an unoccupied bench and sat trying not to think about Joshlyn. Chewing on the inside of her cheek, she thought back on the conversation she found herself having with a complete stranger.

"Excuse me, Miss, is anyone sitting here?" an older gentleman asked.

Kellen pulled her gaze from Chigger and regarded the man. He seemed harmless in a grandpa sort of way. "No, please." Kellen indicated the open part of the bench next to her. "Have a seat."

"Ah, thank you." The man sat and folded the leash in his hands. His fingers and hands were knotted and twisted.

Kellen smiled at the man, but didn't say anything. They sat quietly for a few moments before the man spoke again.

"These old bones can't tolerate standing for very long anymore so I really appreciate you sharing your bench."

"You're welcome." Kellen sensed the man wanted to talk. She wasn't really in the mood to talk, but maybe it was exactly what she needed to get her mind off of her own issues.

Turning towards the man, she crossed her legs and leaned an elbow on the back of the bench. "Are you from around here?"

"Not originally, no. I just recently moved into the assisted living facility across from the park over there," he said, pointing.

"That's a pretty nice place from what I've heard."

"Eh, it's ok."

The man looked at the leash he was twisting in his hands and shook his head. He raised his eyes to Kellen and half smiled.

"I shouldn't complain because I know it's for the best, but when you aren't used to the controlled environment it takes some time to adjust."

"Makes sense," Kellen agreed.

"I lost my wife eight months ago. She was everything to me. When I was diagnosed with Rheumatoid arthritis years ago, she stepped right up and took control of things. If it weren't for her, I don't know how I would have managed. These hands," the man started, holding his hands out in front of him, "well, they just don't function like they used to."

"I'm sorry for your loss," Kellen commented softly. "How long were you married?"

"Fifty-three years. She was my whole world." He stopped to wipe a tear out of the corner of his eye.

"When something's right, it's just right. You don't stop to think about it and by golly, if you have to fight for it then you do."

Kellen turned her head sharply and stared at the man. He couldn't possibly know the situation she was going through, but his words hit their target spot on.

"Did you ever have to fight for her?"

The man chuckled. "Oh my yes. Her father was dead set against us being together and whatever daddy said, went."

Kellen smiled. "So how did you convince her that you were the right one?"

"It wasn't easy, child. She was terrified of her daddy. We spent many years apart before she finally got up the nerve to stand up to him. All I could do was keep trying to convince her that I loved her and we were meant to be together and I'd wait for her."

"What if she had never stood up to him?"

"Then I'd still be fighting to this day. As long as she believed in us then there was always hope."

"How do you know if they believe in what you have?"

"Now that's the question of a lifetime, my dear. Sometimes you don't know, but until you know for sure, then how can you give up?"

"Hmmm," Kellen hummed.

Chigger trotted up, lay down next to Kellen's feet, and closed his eyes.

The man slowly stood. "I best be getting back before they send out a search party. They've got some Nurse Ratchets over there," he said, winking.

Kellen chuckled. "Thank you for the company."

"It was my pleasure." He started for the sidewalk then stopped just as he walked past her. He placed a hand on her shoulder and looked her square in the eyes. "Fight the fight. I promise it's worth it."

❧❧❧❧

Kellen juggled her things and unlocked the sliding door. Dropping her things on the table, she glanced at the clock.

"Fight the fight," she whispered.

That was two days ago and Kellen gave it a lot of thought. Whatever Joshlyn's reasons for breaking off the relationship Kellen wanted to know. She'd been too hurt to question things further that night, but now she was beyond hurt and wanted answers. If she hurried, she would have time to stop by Joshlyn's before getting ready for the race.

❧❧❧❧

Joshlyn pulled the last pictures from the printer and set them down. She slid her chair over and clicked out of the program she was in and back over to her email. She'd spent the better part of two days corresponding with Robin and working out the details for the photos she wanted. Joshlyn decided that maybe getting away and doing this photo opportunity was what she needed. It certainly couldn't hurt things and she could still do the work for Ami because she had two weeks before her deadline was up on those photos.

"One last email and I am done for the night," Joshlyn muttered. She tapped out the message to Robin and sent it off. Closing the programs, she stood and placed her hands at the small of her back. She arched her back, trying to ease the tension and then sighed. Her stomach grumbled loudly, reminding her that she hadn't stopped for lunch earlier.

Joshlyn traipsed down the hall towards the kitchen when the doorbell rang. She glanced down at what she was wearing and groaned. She hadn't bothered to get dressed all day since she had nowhere pressing to be. Her shorts were well worn and you could almost see through her t-shirt. As she got closer to the door, she peeked through the window next to it and saw Kellen's SUV sitting in the drive.

Joshlyn gasped, her heart racing at just the thought of Kellen being on the other side of the door. It wasn't that she hadn't thought about Kellen, but knowing she was just beyond the door and all it took was opening it was more than she could handle. She backed away from the window and leaned against the wall.

The doorbell rang again followed by a couple of short knocks.

"Joshlyn, it's Kellen. Can you please come to the door and talk to me?"

"Just go, Kellen…please," Joshlyn whispered to herself.

Kellen was whispering to herself as well. "C'mon, just open it so we can talk…please, Joshlyn."

Kellen knocked again and leaned close to the door. "Joshlyn, all I'm asking is that you talk to me. I need to understand. I think we can work this out." Kellen listened to see if she could hear any movement inside the house. Joshlyn's car was in the drive, but she could very well be out with Ami.

"Please, Josh," Kellen begged.

Joshlyn stepped close to the door again, but didn't open it. "Kellen, just go, okay? I said all I had to say the other night."

"Can you open the door, please?"

Joshlyn hesitated. "No, I don't think so. I have nothing else to say." Joshlyn's heart ached and her throat felt tight.

Fight the fight. Kellen kept the words going through her head like a mantra. She didn't want to give up, but Joshlyn was making it damned hard.

"Well, I have something to say, Joshlyn. I believe in us and I'm not giving up that easy. I'm giving you fair warning. This isn't over."

Joshlyn gulped, trying to swallow back tears. "It won't change anything, Kellen. Don't waste your time."

"We'll see," Kellen answered.

Kellen stepped back from the door and went back to her SUV. She sat watching the door for a few minutes to see if Joshlyn would open it. When nothing happened, she sighed. She fiddled with her keys and glanced at the mail lying on the seat next to her.

"How did I miss that," Kellen wondered, noticing the plain white envelope addressed to her.

She reached over, took the envelope off the top of the stack, and slid her thumb under the sealed edge. She pulled the letter out and unfolded it, the bold lettering immediately catching her attention.

Heed my warning
Or you'll be sorry

Kellen turned the letter over and then back, looking for something, anything that would give her an idea of who sent it. "What the hell?" She tossed the letter in the seat and drummed her fingers on the steering wheel. There was only one person she could think of that would have any reason to send her a threatening letter and it was about time she let him know she'd had enough.

Kellen started the SUV and headed to the track.

⁕ ⁕ ⁕ ⁕

Joshlyn stood against the wall until she heard Kellen's SUV start. She peered out the window and watched Kellen drive away. Kellen's words definitely made her stumble over her decision to break things off. She had no doubt that Kellen meant what she said. That being the case, Joshlyn really felt she needed to get out of town for a little while. When Kellen came back, she wasn't sure if she would or even could be strong enough not to open the door next time.

Joshlyn fixed herself a sandwich and retreated to her bedroom to pack a bag. She pulled a suitcase from the closet and tossed it on the bed. Haphazardly, she dumped various pieces of clothing from the dresser into the case. She grabbed a couple pairs of slacks off hangers in the closet and folded them into the growing pile. Yanking a sweater from where it hung, she whirled around and almost ran smack into the closet door that had swung partially closed. She pushed the door back open and stopped where she stood. The fractured wooden box caught her attention where it sat on its side with the newspaper article opened underneath it. Up until this point Joshlyn didn't really stop to think about what she was doing, but now she realized that running really wasn't an option. She wasn't experiencing the intense fear that propelled her three years prior. What she did feel was sorrow and hurt.

"What the hell am I going to do?" Joshlyn hollered, throwing her hands in the air.

Chapter Eighteen

Kellen pulled into a parking spot at the track and slammed the SUV into park. The more she thought about the notes, the angrier she became. It wasn't enough that she was dealing with the fallout from Joshlyn dumping her, but to have this bullshit riding her coattails as well was pushing her over the edge. *Enough was fucking enough!* She grabbed her gear and stalked towards the tents, hell-bent on confronting the one person she was sure had a hand in the threatening letters.

Kellen stalked past Emerson's tent, ignoring his hello. Walking right up to her destination, she ripped the tent flap open.

"Where are you?" Kellen growled.

Billy walked around the big toolbox and stood directly in front of Kellen, going toe to toe.

Kellen leaned forward into Billy's personal space. "I'm done with your shit, man." She poked a finger in his chest for emphasis.

"I don't know what the fuck you are talkin' about, Reynolds," Billy sneered.

"I don't take kindly to threats so I suggest you steer clear and back the fuck off!"

"Or what?"

"Don't push me, Billy. You won't like the outcome." Kellen flexed her fists by her side.

"Your threats mean nothin' to me, Reynolds.

Take yer shit and get the hell out of my tent."

Kellen grabbed her bag without taking her eyes off Billy. "I meant what I said, Billy. Back off!" She backed towards the opening of the tent and, with one last look, turned and left.

❧❧❧❧

Billy threw his grease rag against the toolbox and cursed. "Who the fuck does she think she is? She wants to play hard ball, then we'll play hard ball."

Billy hocked a ball of spit to the side and walked over to his car. He was tired of the tiptoeing and acting all buddy buddy as well.

"I'm done with this shit; it's time for that bitch to pay!"

❧❧❧❧

Kellen approached her tent, strolled inside, and threw herself into a chair. Her breathing was rapid and she knew she had to get herself under control. She had never been this angry with anyone in all her life. She clenched and unclenched her hands, willing herself to settle. What she really wanted to do was punch something…or someone. It took every bit of willpower not to put her hands on Billy.

"Hey there, sweetie, you ready for tonight's race?" Bob asked.

Kellen took a couple deep breaths before responding. "You know, Bob, normally I am, but I don't know about this time."

Bob walked over, sat down beside her, and fidgeted with his key ring. "You know, as a rule, I like to stay out of your business, but I am always here for you. Do you want to talk about what's going on, Kellen?"

Kellen leaned forward, resting her arms on her knees, and took a deep breath. "My life was so uncomplicated, Bob. I worked, I raced, and I went home to Chigger."

Bob hesitated before commenting. "And now?"

"Now," Kellen sighed, "Now, I want it to be more complicated and it scares the hell out of me. Joshlyn scares the hell out of me…what she makes me feel."

Kellen stood and paced in front of Bob. "And Billy, that fool doesn't know when to leave well enough alone. Can you believe he has actually been sending me threatening letters?"

"What!" Bob exclaimed, jumping to his feet. "We'll get back to Joshlyn, but I want to deal with Billy first. What did he say?"

"I've gotten two letters telling me to watch my back or someone would stick a knife in it."

"You think he's just trying to scare you or something? I mean, Billy is a coward, we both know that."

Kellen shook her head. "I don't know, Bob. All I know is the last week has been pure hell and I am over it."

"I don't see him doing anything, Kellen, but just watch yourself on the track tonight."

"Oh, I will, don't worry."

Bob nodded and then took a long, hard look at Kellen. "Ok, now you want to talk to me about Joshlyn?"

Kellen started pacing again. "She broke things off with me. I get the feeling she didn't want to and that something scared her. It's just..." Kellen stopped in front of Bob. "I don't know how to get through to her, Bob. She flat won't listen."

"Kellen, I don't have much experience where women are concerned, this much you know. What I can tell you is that sometimes you just have to let things play out as they will."

"I know what you're saying is probably true, but I don't want her to think I am giving up." Kellen sat back down and shifted in her seat so she was facing him. "I *can't* give up on us, Bob. It's right, I can feel it here," Kellen pleaded, patting the left side of her chest.

Bob placed a hand on her knee. "Then all you can do is continue to let her know you are there for her."

Kellen thought a minute before nodding. "You're right."

"Of course I am. Now let's get you ready for time trials!"

"Thanks, Bob. I really appreciate you, ya know?" Kellen wrapped her arms around Bob, startling him.

Bob thumped her on the back a couple times in response and then pulled back, grinning. "C'mon with you, before you make a grown man get all emotional."

Kellen grinned in return and turned to get ready. As soon as she disappeared through the flap, the smile dropped off Bob's face.

"Now what is that little bastard up to?"

❧ ❧ ❧ ❧

Joshlyn picked the remnants of the box up and sat on the edge of her bed. She fingered the yellowed article and looked at the headline again.

TWO ARRESTS IN RACKETEERING CASE
She knew without reading any further that her name would be mentioned and the details of how she turned state's evidence to bust the sting wide open. It also mentioned the threats on her life as well and the one person that still had yet to be captured.

Joshlyn dropped the box and article on the bed and stood up. Maybe if she just told Kellen the truth it would be enough to make her back off on her own.

"That's if she will even talk to me." Josh sighed. The one person she had ever truly connected with and she had treated her like shit. "So what is the worst that could happen? I wouldn't feel any worse than I do now and maybe, just maybe she would understand why I did what I had to do. If we have to go to the police to get protection then we'll just do what we have to do and God help us."

Joshlyn made up her mind and grabbed a jacket and her keys. She glanced at the clock. If she hurried, she might be able to catch Kellen between time trials and the main race.

⁂

Kellen gulped down a mouthful of water as Bob returned with the time trial results.

"Well?"

Bob smiled. "Fourth and even better, Billy is sitting at seventh."

Kellen grunted, but didn't say anything.

"I know, I know," Bob sympathized. "I'm thinking on the positive side here, though."

"I know you are, Bob and I appreciate it. I think I'm going to rest a bit before the race starts."

"I'll holler at you when it's time."

Kellen half-smiled and walked over to the makeshift desk and sat down. She pulled her cell phone out and turned it over in her hand once, twice, and a third time before setting it down. She wanted desperately to call Joshlyn, but on the off chance Joshlyn actually answered, she didn't want their talk time to be limited. Once the race was done for the night, she'd try to call her. For the umpteenth time, Kellen thought back over the night she and Josh went to dinner before the shit hit the fan. It was clear from the get go that Joshlyn was anxious about something, but Kellen chalked it up to meeting Robin. She felt totally blind-sided when Joshlyn said they needed to break things off.

"Hell, the evening wasn't even that bad...was it?" Kellen contemplated to herself.

Kellen wasn't sure how long she sat ruminating, but jerked in surprise when Bob clapped a hand on her shoulder.

"You read to hit the asphalt, kiddo?"

"As ready as I'll ever be, Bobbo." Kellen grinned.

"Bobbo? You're lucky that cute dimple of yours keeps you out of trouble!" Bob threatened.

Kellen laughed and blushed, hopping to her feet. "Let's do this!"

"C'mon, c'mon!" Joshlyn should have known better than to think she could make a quick trip to the track. The traffic was horrendous the closer she got. At this rate, there was no way she was going to get to the track before the race started, much less have a chance to talk to Kellen. Joshlyn had no idea what she was even going to say.

"I can't exactly waltz up and say, 'I was an ass,

please forgive me.' I've got to give her some kind of explanation. Question is, how much do I tell her?" Joshlyn glanced in the rear-view mirror and then back to the road in front of her. Will she even believe me or will she react like everyone else? The friends she thought she had turned on her and she really didn't have a lot of family.

Joshlyn slammed her hand against the steering wheel as traffic came to a complete stop. "Damn!" Slowly the traffic started moving again and Joshlyn was able to turn off on the road that led towards the drivers' tents. Hopefully she would be able to flag someone down that knew her well enough to let her into the area.

She parked, jumped out of the vehicle, and ran towards the gates. Joshlyn tried for over thirty minutes to catch someone's eye with no luck. Just as she was giving up and turned to go, she heard her name being called.

"Joshlyn?" Emerson jogged over to the gate and punched in the code to let her in. "What are you doing here?"

Joshlyn grabbed his arm and squeezed. "Has the race already started?"

"Yeah, they are about fifteen laps into a forty lap race," Emerson explained. "But what are you doing here now? I figured you'd already be down with Bob."

"It's a really long story, Emerson, and I don't have time to get into it. Can you give me a reprieve for now and I'll try to explain later?"

Emerson eyed her for a minute before responding. "Sure. You know where to go?"

"Yes. Thank you, thank you!" Joshlyn started to turn but then stopped. "Hey, why aren't you out there?" She indicted with a tilt of her head towards the track.

"Ah, had a damn engine issue during trials and couldn't get it fixed before the race started."

"Ouch. Sorry to hear that."

Emerson smiled. "Yeah, it'll hurt my points, but not worth what it could cost otherwise."

Joshlyn sympathized. "I completely understand." She turned to look out at the track so she could locate Bob and the crew.

"Go, we can talk more later."

Joshlyn waved and hurried past several tents before hitting the asphalt path to pit road. She crossed the trail, stood behind Kellen's box, and watched as Bob talked to Kellen over the head set.

Bob turned and caught side of Joshlyn. Walking over to her, he raised the microphone and smiled. "Hey there, kiddo. You are a sight for sore eyes."

Joshlyn studied Bob and knew right away that he was aware something had happened between Kellen and herself.

"Bob, I promise when tonight is over, one way or another, there will be some resolution and hopefully Kellen will forgive me."

"I hope so," Bob responded.

Joshlyn flushed but was determined. She had already made up her mind to tell Kellen everything and would let her make her own decisions about where to go from there.

Joshlyn looked out at the track. "So, how is she doing?"

"Everything is running pretty smooth right now. Her timing is good and she's staying away from Billy."

Joshlyn glanced back at Bob. "Something going

on with Billy again?"

"Kellen didn't really go into much detail but she said he had been threatening her, telling her to watch her back."

"What? That is absolutely crazy, Bob. Where does that man get off talking to people like that?"

"Bad blood or no, he is off his rocker with this one," Bob said with a shake of his head. "Listen, I gotta get back on the mic, but hang around. I'm sure Kellen will want to know you are here."

"I'm not going anywhere. I screwed up and it's time I did something about it."

Bob grinned. "Thatta girl!"

Chapter Nineteen

The droning noise of the engine could lull a person to sleep if not careful. Kellen had too much on her mind to be lulled to sleep though. Ten laps to go. Ten more laps and hopefully a top three finish.

"Pffftt," Kellen grunted. What she really wanted was a first place finish again. The high after that race had no comparison…well, almost no comparison. Kellen was not willing to go down that road right now.

"How we doin', Bob?"

"Doin' good, Kellen. You're hauling ass. The 10 car ahead of you is all over the place so watch out for it."

"10-4. You keeping Billy in your sights, Bob? I don't want any surprises from him."

"He's five cars back, Kellen. Just keep your eye on the road and I'll keep my eyes on him. It's all about safety out there."

"I hear ya, Bob." Kellen knew she could trust Bob so she settled back and thought strategy. As it sat right now, she was the third car back. With any luck, she'd make the right moves at the right time and change those statistics. There was a time when she wished her Dad could have been proud of her and proud of what she had accomplished, but that ended a long time ago. She tried, she really did. She never understood what she'd done that was so wrong. Why couldn't he have loved her? Why could she never make him happy? You can't return to the past and change things, but a small part of Kellen sure wished she could. She would have liked to remember more about her mom than little snippets here and there. She knew without a doubt that she resembled her because her father never let her forget that. Any time she would screw up, he'd throw it in her face that she was just like her momma. Lord how she wished she could recall just how like her momma she really was.

"Kellen, head's up. Billy just moved three cars closer to you."

"Thanks, Bob." Kellen glanced in her mirror. "I see him coming." Kellen kept one eye on Billy and the other on the road. Slowly, but surely she could see him making a move to get another car closer. Kellen was stuck behind the 10 car now and knew there was no way around him at this juncture in time. All she could do was hope and pray she could stay away from Billy for another three laps.

⁂

Billy jerked the wheel to the left and put his foot into the gas. He passed the 43 car low on the straightaway. There was no way Kellen was getting around the car in front of her. "That's right, bitch. Yer stuck and all mine!"

Billy was more than aware that Kellen had no idea why he hated her so much. It wasn't that he didn't want to tell her because he'd like nothing more than to smear the truth in her face and watch her crumble. He swore he wouldn't say anything…not that his word was worth much, but it was all about timing. At the right time he'd drop the bomb and watch little miss high and mighty's world come crashing down. Billy laughed outright to himself.

"You just wait. When the time is right I'm gonna enjoy watchin' that light in yer eyes disappear." Billy sneered. He had one more car to pass and then he'd be right where he wanted to be. Slowly Billy pulled up as close to the next car as he could without touching it. He drafted as they got closer to the turn and then shot around the inside, across the edge of the apron, and pulled in front. Now he was exactly where he wanted…no, needed to be. He was going to enjoy this little game before finishing the bitch off.

⚜ ⚜ ⚜ ⚜

"Kellen, Billy's right behind you now. Watch your back!"

"Shit, Bob…what the hell is he up to?" Kellen exclaimed. Her eyes darted from the road to her mirror.

"I don't know, honey, but whatever it is I can't imagine it's any good." Bob chewed his lip and glanced at Joshlyn. She was worried as well so he grabbed her hand and held tight. "She's a good driver. Whatever he's got planned, she'll do her best to avoid it."

Joshlyn nodded but kept silent. She didn't know Billy very well, but knew enough to know that if Bob was worried then there was good reason for it.

"Kellen, he's as close to your bumper as he can be without hitting you."

"I see him, Bob. I can't get around the 10 car or I'd do something about it."

"Just watch your left rear—" Bob stopped talking

all of a sudden.

"I can't shake him, Bob, he's…Oh shit!" Kellen screamed.

Bob watched the scene unfold in front of him as if it were in slow motion. Billy bumped the back left rear of Kellen's bumper and sent her into a spin. The car went towards the apron and then back into oncoming traffic as the driver's side slammed into the wall. The car spun back into the field and was hit by another driver and lifted into the air. It flipped twice before landing on its wheels and slid into the grass before coming to rest.

"Oh my God," Joshlyn whispered.

Bob pulled a trembling Joshlyn into his arms and held her close. "C'mon. Let's get in the truck and get out there."

Joshlyn said a silent prayer as they followed the ambulance out to where Kellen's car was sitting.

❧❧❧❧

Kellen knew the car was sliding out of control and could do nothing to stop it. She tried in vain to steer away from oncoming traffic. As the wall came closer to her side of the car, she threw her left arm up to brace herself. On impact, she felt the bones give way and cried out in response. Her eyes got big when the car drifted back into the line of traffic and she closed them tight when she saw the other car ready to slam into her. Something smashed through the windshield and cracked the face guard on her helmet. The car flipped into the air and on the first contact with the ground Kellen felt a blow to her head and then everything faded to black.

Bob pulled up beside the ambulance and ran to Kellen's car. They already had the netting down and were trying to assess her condition. From what he could see and hear they had removed her helmet because there was so much blood on her face they couldn't see where to stop it. The paramedic had also placed a collar around her neck and an oxygen mask over her nose and mouth.

"Can you tell if she's awake, Bob?" Joshlyn asked.

"Her eyes are closed. I don't think she's awake right now."

The firefighters worked on extricating Kellen from the car so Bob and Joshlyn backed up to give them more room. They slowly slid Kellen onto a hard backboard, strapped her down, and placed her on the stretcher. One of the paramedics was busy starting an IV while another was trying to clean the blood from her face. Once the IV was started, they tried to go to her other hand to start another. Kellen groaned when the paramedic grabbed her wrist.

"We've got a fracture in this wrist. Toss me an arm board." The paramedic secured Kellen's left forearm so it wouldn't get jostled or bumped before an orthopedic doctor could take a look at it.

Kellen fought the fogginess and tried to open her eyes. There was something obscuring her vision so she reached up to move it so she could see what was going on.

"Hang on there, ma'am. We've got some gauze covering your eyes a little because you've got a laceration above your left eye." The paramedic adjusted the gauze some so she could at least see out of one eye.

Kellen dropped her arm back to her chest. "What happened?"

Joshlyn could hear Kellen talking as they wheeled her to the ambulance. She didn't realize how relieved she was until she reached up and wiped the tears from her face. She and Bob followed them to the ambulance and watched as they loaded her inside.

"Where are you taking her?" Bob asked.

"University Hospital, sir."

Bob nodded. "We'll meet you there." He took Joshlyn's arm and headed back to the truck. He waited for her to climb in and closed the door. Once he climbed in himself, he took a deep breath. "Lordy B, what a night!"

"She's going to be all right, don't you think, Bob?" Joshlyn bit her lip and winced. Her hands were still shaking but she felt better knowing that Kellen was awake.

"We'll know more once we get to the hospital, darlin'." Bob patted her hand. "You just hang in there. I have a feeling Kellen's gonna need you once the dust all settles down here."

Joshlyn looked pointedly at Bob before asking, "He did that on purpose, didn't he?"

"I'd like to say no, but I'm afraid it was on purpose. He had no reason to do that; none whatsoever!" Bob started the truck and followed the ambulance out of the speedway.

❧ ❧ ❧ ❧

"How are you doing, ma'am?"

"Please, call me Kellen. My chest hurts a little

and so does my wrist. Otherwise, everything else feels okay. Can you tell me what happened?" Kellen pleaded.

The paramedic recorded the most recent vitals before responding. "You don't remember anything?"

"Oh, I remember the race and then the crash, but after the car flipped it's all a blank." Kellen hesitated before continuing. "Wait a minute, Baker caused that accident, didn't he?"

"I'm not really sure of the details other than I do know your car flipped twice before landing. Sounds like you were only out for about ten minutes total based on what you last remember, though."

Kellen listened to the steady beep of the heart monitor and tried to take shallow breaths. She felt sore overall, but it hurt to take deep breaths. She knew Billy had caused the accident. Him hitting the back of her bumper told her everything she needed to know.

"That son of a bitch," Kellen whispered.

"All right, Kellen, we are pulling into the hospital emergency entrance so it might be a little bumpy for a bit while we get you out and settled into the trauma bay."

"Thank you for everything you've done." Kellen smiled sincerely.

"No worries, you just hang in there."

The paramedic wasn't kidding when he said it was going to be a little bumpy. Kellen held her breath a couple times to keep the pain at a minimum. She knew they were being as gentle as they could, but it still hurt like a son of a bitch. There was so much activity going on around her that Kellen just closed her eyes.

"Ms. Reynolds, I'm Dr. Murphy and we're going to move you from the stretcher to the bed now." Kellen opened her eyes long enough to glance up at who was talking and then closed them again. "On three, guys."

Once they got her moved to the bed, Dr. Murphy started talking to her again and telling her everything they were going to do. "We're just going to roll you up a bit here and check your spine, make sure nothing seems out of place." They rolled her to her right and kept her left arm at her side. "Looks good...roll her back." Someone looked in her eyes and flashed a light in each one.

Kellen groaned. "Feels like you're sticking a hot poker in my eyes."

"I wouldn't be surprised if you've got, at the least, a mild concussion but we'll get a CT scan and make sure nothing else is going on in there. Do you feel nauseated?" Dr. Murphy asked.

"A little bit, yeah."

"How about anything else? Do you hurt anywhere specific?"

"My chest is sore and my left arm hurts," Kellen commented, lifting her arm up a fraction.

Dr. Murphy listened to both sides of her chest and then draped the stethoscope back around his neck. "Breath sounds are good bilaterally. We'll check everything out in CT while up there, but your lungs sound good. As for your arm, you've got a fracture there that we'll get x-rayed and taken care of, too. Are you allergic to anything that you know of, Ms. Reynolds?"

"No, nothing."

"All right, we're gonna give you some Morphine now, which should help with the pain and we'll get you up to CT."

Kellen smiled. "Thanks, doc."

Dr. Murphy smiled down at her. "We'll get you

taken care of here," he said with a wink. "Let's roll, ladies and gentlemen."

❧❧❧❧

Joshlyn couldn't sit still. The doctors had been with Kellen for almost an hour now and nobody had heard a word about Kellen's condition or what was going on. She paced back and forth in front of Bob until he grabbed her hand.

"Have a seat, kiddo. As soon as they have her stabilized and taken care of we'll find out more info."

Joshlyn started to open her mouth, but Bob stopped her with a tug on her arm. She sat down beside him and turned to face him.

"I know it's hard and with the way things are hanging in limbo with you two it makes it even harder." Bob tucked his head so he could get a better look directly into Joshlyn's eyes. "Trust me when I say that things will be okay. Just hang in there a little longer. I called Erin because she's listed on Kellen's 'In Case of Emergency' papers. She'll be here shortly, too."

Joshlyn nodded her head and tried in vain to blink the tears in her eyes away. She swiped a hand across her face and wiped it on her pant leg. Glancing around the waiting room, she realized that she wasn't the only one worried about Kellen's condition. The rest of her crew, Emerson, and the rest of his crew were all sitting and waiting. She'd given Ami a call on her way to the hospital, but she had yet to arrive. The last time Joshlyn had been inside a hospital it was the start of a whole new life for her. She didn't want this time to go down that same road. Joshlyn jerked around in her chair when she heard rapid footsteps coming her way from down the hall. She stood as Ami rounded the corner.

Ami pulled Joshlyn into a hug. "What on earth happened?" She leaned back and looked at Joshlyn.

"There was an accident at the track. We still don't know much of anything other than she was awake and talking when they put her into the ambulance."

Emerson walked over to stand beside his sister and gave Joshlyn a supportive smile. "Hey, sis."

"Hey, Em. Sorry I got here so late, guys. I had to drop Jaxon off at the airport."

Joshlyn leaned into Ami for warmth and support. "I'm just glad you're here now. Thank you so much for coming."

"Hey, I'd have been upset with you if you hadn't called me. Do you all need coffee or anything while we wait?" Ami wrapped her arm around Joshlyn and walked her over to sit down.

"I'm good, thanks though, Ami." Joshlyn rubbed her hands together and smiled. She was so thankful to be here with people who cared…not just for Kellen but for herself as well.

Emerson pulled a chair closer to Ami, Joshlyn, and Bob and leaned in a little. "Bob, what's the deal with Billy? They stopped the race completely and when we left the track they were questioning him."

"Em, I'm telling you that boy was a menace from the get go, but tonight took the cake. I think one of the other guys must have told the officials what we suspected. I wouldn't be surprised if he gets some sort of charges filed on him for this one."

"Can they prove it?"

"All they gotta do is look at the tapes. The proof is right there in front of their noses. It's crazy, but after all this time—" Bob stopped abruptly when the doctor from the trauma room came walking around the corner.

"Family for Kellen Reynolds."

Joshlyn jumped to her feet as well as Emerson, Bob, and Ami. "That's us."

Just before the doctor started to speak, a small auburn-haired woman raced up to the group and enveloped Bob in a hug. Joshlyn assumed this had to be Erin. Bob gave her a one armed hug and they both turned towards the doctor.

Dr. Murphy pulled his surgical cap off and ran a hand through his hair. "All her tests are back and they look good. I don't see any need for any type of surgery. She's a very lucky woman, though. Her ribs and sternum are bruised so she'll be sore for a few days with that. We stitched the laceration through her left eyebrow and forehead. She didn't have any debris inside the cut so best we can figure is that the shield from her helmet impacted that area and caused the laceration. She has a mild concussion for which we are going to keep her at least overnight and reevaluate her tomorrow. The biggest issue is the fracture to her left wrist. She's going to be out of commission with that for at least six to eight weeks. As I said, overall she is a very lucky woman. Any questions?"

Joshlyn stepped forward a little. "When can we see her, doctor?"

"They are getting her settled in a room and then you can have a brief visit. I want her to get some rest tonight. If you'll follow me I'll show you to the waiting room on the unit."

Kellen struggled to get comfortable. It didn't matter which way she turned because at this moment it seemed her entire body was one big bruise. She finally gave up and blew an exasperated breath out. Luckily, she didn't have a roommate. According to her nurse on duty, almost all the rooms were private now. She glanced around the room and sighed. The doctor explained that the splint on her left wrist would be removed in a couple days and a real cast would be put in place as soon as the swelling had gone down. By tomorrow her left eye would look like she went a few rounds in a boxing ring. It was already swollen and tender. She was reaching towards it when there was a quiet knock on her door. She didn't answer but waited for the door to open.

Bob opened the door slowly in case Kellen was asleep. When he peeked through the opening, he could see Kellen and she was giving him a lop-sided grin. "Hey there, kiddo." Bob and Erin walked further into the room and stood next to the bed. "How ya doin?"

"You mean aside from looking like hell?" Kellen chuckled and groaned. "Oh, don't make me laugh. Right now everything hurts."

"You scared the shit out of me, girl." Bob smiled affectionately down at Kellen. He placed a hand on her arm and rubbed lightly. "Don't ever do that again!"

"Bob, I can guarantee you it wasn't on my agenda tonight. Speaking of, please tell me that someone else saw that Billy was responsible this time?"

"Honey, when the boys left the track the police already had Billy aside and were questioning him. At this point I have no idea what is going on because we've all been here since you came in."

"Are you kidding me? Bob, tell them all to go home. I'm fine!"

"Kellen, when are you going to learn that we all consider you family? I'm not just talking about me and the crew. I'm talking about Emerson and his boys, too. Ami is out there as well." Bob purposefully didn't mention Joshlyn. Right now, he wanted to keep Kellen's emotions at a minimum.

Kellen didn't even bother trying to hide the tears welling up in her eyes. "I…ahem…I'm sorry, Bob."

"Don't be sorry. Just know we all care very much for you. I'm gonna get on outta here, but are you up for one more visitor?"

"Sure."

"All right then. I'm going to go by and check on Chigger, but I'll be back tomorrow. Sleep well."

Kellen smiled at Bob as he left and cleared her throat. She wasn't used to fighting down this much emotion. Hell, Bob probably wouldn't know what to do with her if she'd gone into a full-blown crying jag. The thought made her smile again. She glanced back over where Erin quietly stood.

"Hey, Erin. Why are you being so quiet? I don't think I've ever heard you not say anything for this long."

"Very funny, woman," Erin replied, wiping a tear from her cheek. "You scared the shit out of me!"

"I'm sorry, Erin. I promise I didn't do this on purpose."

"I know, honey. I've already talked to Bob as we were walking in here." Erin stopped briefly when the door started to open. "Listen, I'm going to head out, but you need anything you call, okay?"

"Okay, thank you, Erin."

"Any time, sweetheart." Erin leaned down and kissed her on the forehead. She smiled at Joshlyn on the way out.

Joshlyn stepped into the room, smiled at Erin in return, and walked straight up to Kellen's bed. Even with all the bumps and bruises, she was still the most beautiful person Josh had ever seen. All Kellen could do was look at her so Joshlyn decided to just jump right in.

"I'm so sorry, Kellen," Joshlyn whispered. "I know you have no right to forgive me for what I said and did, but I hope once you are home that you will let me explain or at least hear me out. Once I do, if you never want to see me again I will totally understand."

Kellen didn't say anything, but continued to stare. Joshlyn knew she had to still be upset over everything, but was hoping Kellen would talk to her some. When she made no effort, a sob broke free from Joshlyn and she put a hand to her mouth to try to tamp it down.

Kellen's resolve broke and she reached out with her good hand. "Ssshhh, Josh, right now all I care about is that you are here. I'm very happy to see you despite the reason behind it. Or maybe I should say in spite of, huh?"

Joshlyn gave her a watery smile and gently took her hand. "I was so scared when you hit that wall, Kellen. I don't think I've ever been more scared in my entire life."

"You were there? You saw what happened?"

"Oh yeah, I wanted to get there between time trials and the start of the race, but alas, traffic was not cooperating. I wanted to explain some things to you then."

"Josh, when I get home I will most definitely

listen to what you have to say, but you also have to listen to me and hear me out."

Joshlyn studied Kellen for a minute before responding. "Okay, I can do that. Fair is fair. Right now though, you look like it's taking everything you have to stay awake. Why don't you go ahead and rest and we can talk more later."

"I, uh, please don't go yet...please?" Kellen grasped Joshlyn's hand tighter.

"I won't. Go ahead and close your eyes. I'll be here. I'm just going to pull this chair closer."

"Will you lean close for just a minute?"

Joshlyn moved up closer to the head of the bed and leaned down. "What is it?"

"Thank you. Thank you so much for being here," Kellen raised her head a bit and kissed Joshlyn's cheek.

"Oh honey, there's no place else I'd rather be. Wherever you are is where I want to be." Joshlyn placed her palm against the side of Kellen's cheek and kissed her lightly on the lips. "Now rest before the nurses come in and throw me out."

Kellen grinned. "Yes ma'am."

Joshlyn pulled the chair closer, sat down, and reached for Kellen's hand again. Kellen's eyes closed before Joshlyn even got the chair back by the bed. She rubbed her thumb lightly over the back of Kellen's hand. The worst possible scenario could have happened tonight, but Joshlyn was so thankful it didn't. At least now she'd have the opportunity to tell Kellen everything. Then she could make her own decision about whether to stick around or not. It wasn't going to be easy, but by the grace of luck, maybe she could finally really settle down and not look over her shoulder all the time.

Chapter Twenty

Two days, well, actually thirty-eight hours, seem to drag on forever for Kellen. She was more than ready to get out of this hospital room and back to her own house. Not to mention she was missing Chigger like crazy. Joshlyn was supposed to be by within the hour to pick her up and it couldn't come soon enough. Kellen had a lot of time to think over the last day or so and came to the decision that, no matter what Joshlyn had to say, they would work things out...one way or the other. Whatever Joshlyn had to say Kellen knew it was something big. Why else would she have pushed her away? Kellen couldn't stop loving Joshlyn if she tried and all she had to do was figure out a way to convince her that she really meant it.

"Love?" Kellen whispered. Her stomach was full of butterflies and her heart felt like it was going to beat out of her chest. She took a deep breath and glanced out the window. Is it possible that what she felt was love? Kellen wasn't sure she had ever been truly in love with anyone before. Sure, she had relationships, but none of those ever compared to the feelings she had for Joshlyn. Kellen wanted to dissect everything further, but the knock on her door meant it would have to be later.

Joshlyn pushed the door open and smiled. "Hey there. How are you feeling? Ready to blow this popsicle stand?"

"Uh, yeah," Kellen said, clearing her throat. "Yeah, I'm more than ready."

Joshlyn studied Kellen fidgeting with the splint on her arm and tilted her head a little. "Everything okay in here?"

Kellen brought her eyes up to Joshlyn's and everything else around her seemed to fade away. The sparkle in Josh's eyes, the easy smile on her lips, the way the edges of her eyes crinkled when she did smile, and the way she smelled…all of it. Kellen gave an appreciative sigh.

Joshlyn chuckled. "What was that big sigh for?"

"I'm just really, really glad you're here, Josh. Thank you."

"It's no problem, Kel. C'mon, if you're all ready let's get your stuff loaded up and give the nurse a buzz."

"Everything is ready to go." Kellen pushed the call button for the nurse. "Can you come here a second?"

Joshlyn stepped closer and clasped her fingers around Kellen's. "What's up?"

Kellen lowered her voice and leaned forward. "Nothing, I just wanted to do this." She lightly brushed her lips across Joshlyn's once and then again. Just as she was pulling away, Joshlyn reached up and pulled her back again. Kellen moistened her lips seconds before Joshlyn claimed them again and deepened the already consuming kiss. Time seemed to disappear and before either of them knew it, someone was clearing their throat.

Joshlyn placed her forehead against Kellen's. "Yeah, let's get out of here."

Kellen smiled at Joshlyn's flushed appearance and peeked over at the nurse. "I'm ready whenever you ladies give the word." She stood gingerly, pivoted, and sat back down in the wheelchair.

⁂

Once they got back to Kellen's house, Joshlyn let Chigger out and set about making Kellen a little more comfortable.

"I really appreciate you and Bob taking care of Chigger the last couple days."

"Oh, it was not a problem at all. He is such a good boy. I think he really missed you though; seems like he barely touched his food."

"Poor buddy, he probably felt like I had abandoned him. Any time I go away for a short period of time he gets a little nervous. He'll be okay, just might take him a day or so to settle back down."

"Can I get you something to drink? You might want to go ahead and take one of those pills they sent home with you."

"Sure. I know I'm supposed to stay clear of coffee for a little bit, but do you think you could make some of that decaf that's in the cabinet?"

"You bet. I'll be back in just a minute."

Joshlyn filled the machine with water and dropped some decaf grounds in the basket. While it brewed, she leaned against the counter and ran a finger over her lips. Something was different about Kellen… or maybe there was something different about her. The emotions she felt in that kiss were a lot different from what she had felt in the past. It's not that she didn't enjoy kissing Kellen because that had always been pretty spectacular between the two of them. Josh got the impression there was more substance between them in just that one kiss. *That one really deep, really hot kiss!* Joshlyn grinned and walked over to let Chigger back in from his outside exploring. She fixed herself and Kellen a cup of coffee and headed back into the living room. Hopefully there would be plenty of time to figure out what all these new feelings and sensations were all about.

"Here ya go."

Kellen took the cup from Joshlyn and brought it to her nose. "Mmm, God that smells terrific." She took a small sip and groaned in pleasure. "Thank you! That tastes so good."

Joshlyn sat in the chair perpendicular to Kellen, took a sip of her coffee, and set it down. She chewed her lip a little and took a deep breath. "Kellen, I'm not sure if you are ready to get into this or not, but I would really like the opportunity to explain some things to you if you are up to it."

"Josh, before you say anything, I just want you to understand that whatever it is we'll work through it, okay?"

"I appreciate you saying that, but just know I'm not holding you to that. Once I tell you what I have to say, you are free to make your own decisions. Can we leave it at that?"

Kellen held Joshlyn's eyes for a minute before nodding in defeat. "For now."

"Okay, well, what I'm about to tell you is something I haven't told anyone. I gave Ami a few details, but she knows nothing about what I'm going to tell you."

"Whatever you tell me is between us, Josh. I

won't tell anyone unless you specifically want me to."

"Thank you, I appreciate that. Three years ago, everything you know about me was a lot different. I worked for a medical equipment company. I pretty much did everything that involved the money. Three brothers and their sister owned the company and they were in charge of bringing in new contracts and finding new contacts. I hadn't even worked there a year before Candace, the sister, and I got involved. Maybe six months after that, I started noticing some inconsistencies in some of the numbers. Insurance companies were being billed for equipment I wasn't aware we even had. Eventually I started looking into some of the statements. One thing led to another and I came across a whole hornet's nest worth of trouble. They were having me bill insurance companies for products that were supposedly being sent out to people who needed them, but it was never happening. I started a paper trail of everything that was going on. For six more months, I copied and compared every single statement and payment that went out or came in. It didn't take long for me to realize that what they were up to was highly illegal and that I needed to do something and fast. I went to Candace first about it, but it was clear that she was in on it as well when she tried to convince me I was making mistakes and to leave it alone and she'd take care of it. Eventually I went to the police, who turned it over to the FBI. I agreed to confront them all while wearing a wire and in return they wouldn't charge me as an accomplice."

"Wait, why would they charge you as an accomplice?"

"Because I was the one in charge of the books, Kellen. It's my name on those invoices and my name that came across on the checks. For all intents and purposes it makes me look like the guilty one."

"That's insane!"

"Be that as it may, I wasn't about to go down for something I had not been a part of, nor would I ever be. I wore the wire and confronted them. Needless to say, they were shocked. For whatever reason, they thought I didn't and wouldn't check the books. Things didn't go very well from there. They admitted to everything and even went so far as to blame Candace because she was supposed to keep me otherwise occupied. The FBI busted in after they had it all on tape. One brother ran but was taken down fairly quickly. He turned a gun on them and they shot and killed him. The other grabbed me and held a gun to my head—"

"Oh my God, Josh, you could have been killed!" Kellen's hands trembled as she set her cup down.

Joshlyn watched as Kellen's color turned pallid. She jumped up and moved over to sit by Kellen. She turned so one leg was resting on the couch and took Kellen's clammy hands in her own. "Sweetheart, I had to do it, don't you understand? As long as I kept silent, people were being robbed of the equipment they truly needed. Not to mention my own name was being slung through the mud."

"I understand, Josh, I really do, it's just the thought of them hurting you or even holding a gun to your head makes me physically sick to my stomach."

"I love you, you know that?" Joshlyn grinned as Kellen's eyes got huge and her mouth dropped open. "I know, hell of a time for admissions, huh?" Joshlyn shrugged. "What can I say?"

Before Kellen could say anything, Joshlyn went on. "Anyhow, the brother holding the gun to my head wasn't very smart. He had no idea what to do or where to go. He didn't make it far. He shoved me at Candace and tried to run, but they took him out in nothing flat when he tried to shoot one of their agents. Candace had a knife against my neck and started pulling me away towards a side door. Things got a little confusing at this point because it was so chaotic. I am only able to tell you this part because it's what I was told. They knew if Candace got out the door they'd never get me back alive so they took her out. A sharpshooter shot her and in the process, she fell forward against me and I hit the side of my head against a pallet of equipment that knocked me out cold. I fell on her knife and it went into my shoulder. The third brother was a different story. Unfortunately, to this day they still haven't caught him. Before I go on, do you need anything?"

"A glass of water? All of a sudden I am parched as can be."

"It's probably the medicine." Joshlyn grabbed a glass of water and waited for Kellen to drink some before sitting back down. "You good or need some more?"

"Nah, I'm good, thanks." Kellen took Joshlyn's hand again and waited for her to continue.

"When all of this hit the papers, the few friends I had didn't know what to believe. My name was linked with everything. I guess that should have been my first clue. Real friends wouldn't have turned tail and run at the first indication of trouble, but in the crowd my family was involved in, I shouldn't have been surprised at their actions. Heaven forbid they should be linked with anyone that might be shady. I had one really good friend, Lori, that stuck by me through everything. My mother and I were not close after I came out to her. My father passed away a couple years before this all happened. Because I was the youngest, my sisters were always jealous of me, so when I came out they were overjoyed to be getting all of my mother's attention. I did become pretty good friends with one of the FBI agents through the whole ordeal. I'm kind of getting off track here a little bit so let me back up. Essentially, what I'm telling you is that I didn't have hardly anyone to turn to when I needed it. A week or so after this all went down I started getting hang up phone calls. First, it was just at home and then I started getting them on my cell. I went to Sydney, the FBI agent I was telling you about, and told her what was going on. She said they could put a tap on the phone, but if I couldn't keep the person on the phone, it wouldn't do much good. Then I started getting threatening letters in the mail."

"What kind of threatening letters?"

"The kind that said, 'You're dead bitch!' and also that 'You better watch your back.'"

"Josh, I think you should know that I've been getting threatening letters."

"What? What do you mean? What kind of threatening letters?"

"I've got them around here somewhere. Check over there on the entertainment system, would you?"

Joshlyn jumped up, hurried over to the entertainment center, and rifled through the mail. Right there in the middle was an open letter. She pulled it out, unfolded it all the way, and read it. "He's found me, Kellen, and he knows about you. This has to be from him!"

"Come back over here and sit down. We'll get

this figured out. Can you give Sydney a call and see if she's heard anything?"

"Yeah, hang on." Joshlyn pulled her cell from her pocket and punched in Sydney's number. It rang and rang and then went to voicemail. "Sydney, this is Joshlyn. Give me a call as soon as you get this message. Some things have been going on and I really need to talk to you." She hung up the phone and stood. She paced back and forth in front of Kellen before Kellen finally grabbed her hand.

"Honey, sit down. You're making me dizzy. We'll just stick together until we hear from Sydney and if need be, we'll call the police."

"Kellen, don't you see?" Joshlyn jerked her hand away from Kellen. "The police can't do anything about it. We can't even prove it's him. I should get away from you. If he wants me, then he can come get me, but I will not involve you in this. I couldn't stand it if anything happened to you."

"Joshlyn…Josh! Stop. He already knows about me. You being away from me isn't going to matter. Quite honestly, it's not what I want either. We'll handle this together; hopefully once and for all."

"I am so sorry, Kellen. I never meant for you to get pulled into this. That's why I broke things off. When Robin said she saw the newscast nationally, I completely freaked out."

"Josh, please sit down for a minute." As soon as Joshlyn sat down, Kellen continued. "I completely understand why you would be upset about this and I would have freaked out as well. You don't have to do it alone. Promise me you'll never shut me out like that again?"

"Kellen, I can't promise you that I won't make

mistakes again, but I can promise you that I will do everything in my power to never make you feel that way again. I am sorrier than I can even say…I don't know how you can forgive me."

"Josh, I can forgive you because I love you, too. As long as we communicate then we can work through almost anything."

Joshlyn threw herself into Kellen's arms and then pulled away almost as quickly when Kellen groaned. "Oh my gosh, I am so sorry, Kel. Damn, I keep hurting you!"

Kellen put a finger to Josh's lips. "Ssshhh. Don't apologize. Just take it a little slower next time." Kellen grinned and pulled Joshlyn into her arms. They sat like that for some time before Joshlyn pulled away a little.

"I think there's only one more thing I need to tell…well, show you and then there are no more secrets."

"Oookay…"

Joshlyn turned and ducked her head a bit before turning back towards Kellen. She raised her head and looked straight into Kellen's eyes.

"Holy shit!" Kellen exclaimed. "Your eyes…they are absolutely gorgeous! Josh, why would you hide those beautiful green eyes?"

"Once the threatening letters started coming, Sydney got really concerned. One day while we were out to lunch, a small pipe bomb went off in my apartment. The FBI took advantage of that and put out headlines saying I had been a victim and unfortunately could not be saved. From that point on, I ceased to exist. I dropped all contact with my best friend and what family I had. I became a whole new person. Hence the reason I covered my eyes with those contacts. There is no way I could hide these bright green babies from anyone. It was always the one feature that made me stand out."

"I can see why. So, can you tell me what your name was before?"

Joshlyn hesitated. She hadn't uttered that name in almost three years. She didn't see herself as that person anymore and really didn't want Kellen to associate her with that name either.

"Joshlyn, no matter what you tell me you will always be Josh to me. I hope that's okay?"

Joshlyn smiled at Kellen and nodded. "That is more than okay. My previous name was Jeri Denton."

Kellen considered the name for a minute and shook her head. "I don't see you as a Jeri. Sorry, but I just don't."

Josh laughed and hugged Kellen lightly. "You know, at one time I might have been offended by that, but now, it's perfect."

"Since the cat is out of the bag, so to speak, do you think you could leave the contacts out now?"

"I could do that, if you want."

"I want, I really, really want."

"Kellen, I meant what I said earlier. I really do love you. I'm so in love with you it scares me."

"We're in the same boat, honey, because I am very much in love with you as well. I know now that I have never been truly in love with anyone in my entire life. It scares and exhilarates me all at once."

Joshlyn raised her head to look up at Kellen. "So, how are you feeling?"

"I feel good enough to retreat to the bedroom if that is what you're asking," Kellen teased, wiggling her eyebrows in Josh's direction.

Joshlyn laughed and stood. She held a hand out to help Kellen up off the couch. "How about we retreat to the bedroom and once we get you settled, we'll see just how well you feel."

Kellen smacked Josh lightly on the backside and leaned close to her ear. "Lead on, sexy."

Chapter Twenty-one

Joshlyn stopped near the bed and took Kellen's hand in her own. She placed her other hand above the splint and pulled Kellen closer, close enough they were almost touching. "I love you, Kellen, and I can't tell you how afraid I was of almost losing you." Kellen was opening her mouth to respond but Joshlyn shook her head. "Let me finish. I almost lost you and I was such a creep to you. I can't tell you how I felt when I saw you hit that wall. I'm very thankful to be getting this second chance with you and I will do everything in my power to make it up to you."

"Can I speak now?"

Joshlyn smiled and nodded.

"You don't need to make anything up to me, Josh. All I need is for you to love me."

"Oh honey, loving you has never been a problem and right now I'm about to love you completely," Joshlyn stated firmly, her voice lowering a notch.

Joshlyn slid her hands up Kellen's arms, across her shoulders, and placed her palms on each side of her face. Gently she pulled Kellen to her and nipped lightly at her lips. Kellen's breath came out in a rush and Josh heard her moan. She ran her tongue across Kellen's lips and then took her mouth in a deep, searing kiss. When she couldn't breathe any longer, she pulled away. Kellen's lips were swollen and her eyes were glazed.

"God, Kellen, you are so damn beautiful. You take my breath away."

Joshlyn's eyes darted back and forth between Kellen's. Those bright blue eyes were now full of tears. "You make my heart hurt, but in a good way."

Kellen smiled and hastily wiped her eyes clear. "How is a girl supposed to compete with those kinds of words, huh?"

"There is no competing with the truth, honey." Joshlyn slid her hands down across the front of Kellen's shirt. Her hands crept up under the edge of the shirt and grazed softly across Kellen's stomach.

"Good grief, woman, you are about to drive me nuts!" Kellen groaned and closed her eyes. The sensation made the hairs on her arms stand up and her pelvis grow instantly warm.

Joshlyn leaned in, kissed the open expanse of chest between Kellen's collarbones, and brought one hand up to unbutton her shirt. With each button she released, she kissed the new area exposed. As the last button released, Josh ran her tongue around Kellen's navel and nipped at it with her teeth. The second time she nibbled at the skin around her navel, Kellen's hand went into Josh's hair and held her close.

"Come here, Josh."

Joshlyn straightened back up without dislodging Kellen's hand from hair. "Yessss?"

Kellen claimed Josh's lips again and fought for control. She walked Joshlyn to the edge of the bed and sat them both down without ending the kiss. She couldn't get close enough. Joshlyn wrenched her lips free and gasped.

"Stand up a second, Kellen, and let me get those trousers off you."

Kellen stood patiently while Josh unbuttoned her pants and lowered them and her briefs to the ground. Then Josh stood and lowered the shirt off her shoulders and down her arms, taking extra care when it caught on the splint. She wasn't wearing a bra since she got dressed before Joshlyn got to the hospital. She couldn't clasp the damn thing anyhow. Once everything was off, she sat back down.

Joshlyn started to lift her shirt when she saw Kellen smirk. "What?"

"Oh, don't mind me, I'm just going to sit here and watch the show."

Joshlyn reached down and pulled the shirt slowly over her head. Pulling her hair free, she threw the shirt to the side. She reached behind to unclasp her bra and slid the straps ever so gently down her arms before letting it drop to the floor as well. Her thumb and finger flicked the snap open on her jeans and she casually lowered the zipper.

"Joshlyn…" Kellen growled.

Joshlyn grinned while slipping her fingers inside the waistband of her jeans, lowered them and her panties down her legs, and kicked them to the side. She moved back next to Kellen.

"Lay down, honey."

Once Kellen was lying flat, Joshlyn went around to the other side of the bed and crawled under the covers. She scooted closer and raised Kellen's left arm above her head onto the pillow. "Just keep that arm up there. I don't want to take a chance of bumping it."

They both leaned in at the same time, uncharacteristically bumping into each other. Kellen laughed and pulled back. "Stay right there." Kellen leaned forward then and kissed Josh on the lips, moved down and placed a small peck on her chin. Lifting her head, she placed light butterfly kisses on each eyelid.

"Mmm, Kellen, as much as I love what you are doing and please don't get me wrong, I really do love it. However, I need you…I want to crawl inside you and never leave."

"There you go again with those words—"

Kellen didn't get to finish her sentence because Joshlyn put a finger to her lips, pushed her onto her back, and was now settled across her hips.

"I'm done talking, Kellen. I want to show you."

"Not arguing…not talking."

Joshlyn leaned forward and kissed the space between Kellen's breasts before moving over to take a nipple in her mouth. She swirled her tongue around the turgid flesh and sucked gently. Releasing Kellen's nipple, she kissed lower down her abdomen until she reached the apex of her legs. Kellen's legs automatically spread further apart to give her room. Josh caressed up the inside of both thighs before spreading Kellen open and taking her in her mouth.

Kellen arched under the contact and immediately felt herself grow even wetter. She gasped aloud when Joshlyn flicked her tongue across her clit. Her hips started moving in time with Josh's mouth.

"Oh God, baby, that feels so good," Kellen cried out as she felt the pressure grow inside her. She knew she was on the verge of release.

"I'm so close, honey, so so close."

Joshlyn increased her tempo and slid two fingers inside. Kellen moaned and her body went rigid as the climax overtook her. Kellen's body went limp and her breathing was very ragged.

"Oh, Josh," was all she could utter.

Joshlyn kissed the inside of a thigh and then moved up to lie on her side next to Kellen and pulled the covers up over them. She curled an arm below Kellen's breasts and felt a fine sheen of sweat that covered her entire body.

"You completely destroy me, Josh. You'll have to give me a minute to reciprocate, honey." Kellen's pulse was finally slowing down and her breathing had evened out.

"Just rest, Kel. We've got all the time in the world."

Kellen beamed. "Thank you for coming into my life." She leaned forward, kissed Joshlyn on the cheek, and then closed her eyes with her head resting against Josh's.

Thank YOU for coming into my life, Kellen Reynolds. Joshlyn released a contented sigh and closed her eyes as well. Before long, they were both fast asleep.

❧ ❧ ❧ ❧

"How many eggs do you want, hon?" Joshlyn shouted from the kitchen.

Kellen grinned from her spot against the kitchen doorway. "You don't have to shout, I'm right here."

Joshlyn jumped. "Damn, you scared me!"

Kellen chuckled. "I'll take two eggs, but you know you don't have to do that."

"I know, but I want to." Joshlyn walked over, leaned in, and kissed Kellen. "Now, why don't you go sit down? Want to eat here or in the living room?"

"Hm, how about here? Just holler when you're ready."

Joshlyn hummed while fixing the eggs. She

loved the whole feeling of domestication with Kellen. It was something she could definitely get used to. Hours after they fell asleep the previous night, Joshlyn awoke still in the same position they had fallen asleep. She tilted her head back and just stared at Kellen. The complications of life faded away and all she could see was a bright future with Kellen…it's all she ever wanted, to feel like she had a home and had someone's heart. From the long conversations she and Kellen shared, it was obvious that this is what Kellen wanted as well. There were past relationships, albeit many years ago, but none ever made her feel complete, safe, and secure. She always had this feeling of being lost that she chalked up to the investigation and everything that followed in the aftermath. Now that she had it within her means, she'd be damned if she'd give it up without a fight. She nodded to herself and slid the eggs onto each plate. Grabbing some tongs, she dropped a couple pieces of turkey sausage and some toast as well. She picked up the plates and headed to the living room.

❧❧❧❧

Kellen sat back and groaned. "That was great, Josh. Thank you."

"It really was no big deal, hon."

"I know, but I appreciate the effort and that you wanted to do it."

Joshlyn was getting ready to respond when her cell phone rang. Leaning forward, she picked it up. "It's Sydney," she said, already pushing the talk button. "Hey, Syd, I know you've been trying to get ahold of me and I'm sorry I haven't returned your calls." Josh hoped to head Sydney off at the pass before she could chastise her for not calling back sooner.

"Listen, it's ok, but I really need to talk to you."

"I need to talk to you as well. Do you know—"

Sydney stopped her before she could say anything else. *"Hey, what I need to talk to you about I'd really rather do in person. Can you hold off long enough for me to get there?"*

Joshlyn's brow furrowed. "Um, yeah, I guess. How long before you can be here?"

"Give me a couple hours, shouldn't take any longer than that."

"Ok, I'll see you then."

"I'll see you soon. And Joshlyn, thanks for finally returning my calls!"

Sydney had already hung up before Joshlyn could respond. She set her phone back down.

"Everything okay?"

Joshlyn sucked a lip into her mouth and released it before answering. "Yeah, I think so. She said she wants to talk to me, but would rather do it in person. She should be here in a couple hours."

"What do you think she needs to talk to you about?"

"Well, based on the threats you've been getting I'm almost afraid to speculate. I think…no, I'm afraid that she's going to tell me that I've been found. What else could it be, Kel?"

"Honey, there's no use in getting yourself worked up just yet. Let's find out what she has to say and we'll go from there."

"How can you sit there and be so calm about this. Your life has been threatened! Don't you get it? These guys meant business, Kellen, and now that two of them are gone if you think he has anything to lose at this point by coming here you're wrong!" Joshlyn stood and took their plates to the kitchen.

Kellen took a deep breath and let it out. Honestly, she was just as concerned that *both* their lives were in danger. Actually, she was scared to death, not so much for herself but for Josh. She'd do anything to protect her and by acting like it was no big deal she inadvertently pushed her away. She hoped Sydney got here sooner rather than later because at this point she was ready just to go to the police and let them take care of whatever was happening. Her initial feelings were that Billy was the person responsible for the threatening letters. He always had some type of vendetta against her. So much so that she couldn't even remember what started it and this was long before the accident that took Peetie's life. No matter how she played it out in her head, she always came up with the same results. Billy.

Kellen was about to get up and go find Josh when she came back into the living room.

"Hey, listen, it's not that—"

"Look, I'm sorry for being—"

Joshlyn stopped. "You go ahead."

"I was just going to say that it's not that I don't think they or I should say he doesn't mean business, I know he does. I'm just trying to stay positive for you and keep your anxiety level down. The last thing you need is for me to be a nervous Nelly about it all, too."

"I know, Kel. I get it and I'm sorry for being such a bitch. It's not just about me anymore. I could handle it easier if it were."

"Hence the reason you pushed me away and ended things. I don't normally scare easily, Josh, especially when someone I love is involved."

Joshlyn smiled lovingly. "Yeah, I got that." Kellen laughed outright and patted the spot on the couch next to her.

Joshlyn sat down and leaned against Kellen's shoulder. "I don't want you hurt anymore, Kellen."

"Hey, look at me." Kellen waited for her to sit up and then turned sideways on the couch to face Joshlyn and took a hand in her own. "Whatever happens, we are in this together. Got me?"

Joshlyn hesitated. Kellen made it sound so simple. She ran her palm down Kellen's cheek, traced her lower lip, and then tapped it. "Got it." She gently probed the puckered skin around the stitches running through Kellen's eyebrow and winced. "How's that feeling?"

"Actually I don't even notice it's there except the fact it itches so much."

Joshlyn was about to suggest some lotion when the doorbell rang. She looked at her watch and glanced at Kellen. "She got here fast."

Kellen stood. "I'll get it." She traipsed over to the front door and unlocked it. She smiled over at Joshlyn and then opened the door.

Joshlyn saw Kellen visibly pale and grab the doorframe.

"What..." Kellen started. "What are you doing here?"

Chapter Twenty-two

Aren't you even going to invite me in?"
Kellen just stared. The myriad of feelings racing through her were way too intense. How? When? Why? She wanted to ask all these questions and more, but couldn't find the words. Instead, she just stared.

"Kellen?" Joshlyn was getting worried when Kellen just stood there. She could see her trembling and the color had yet to return so she stood up.

Kellen put a hand up. "Stay there, Josh," she said without looking at her. "What do you want, Jeff?" Kellen heard Josh gasp, but continued to look at Jeff.

"What I want is for you to invite your dear old dad inside."

"Not gonna happen. Not now, not ever."

Jeff glowered. "You coulda made this so much easier. You remember that later." He pulled a gun from behind his back and pointed it at her. "Now, get inside."

Kellen stepped back and allowed him inside the house. He slammed the door shut and motioned for her to sit down. Chigger picked that moment to start barking at Jeff.

"Shut that damn dog up!"

"Chigger, come here boy, c'mon." Chigger ignored her and kept barking.

Jeff turned towards the dog and swung his foot at him, catching him in the hindquarter. Chigger yelped and ran to the bedroom. He grumbled and looked back at Kellen. She was mad now, which was good. "Now, you're gonna listen to me and do what I say, right?"

"What do you want, Jeff?" Kellen was seething on the inside. The two things in this world that she was protective about were Chigger and Joshlyn. Her blood was boiling. All she wanted to do was beat the hell out of Jeff, but in her condition, it wasn't going to happen. *Damn him!*

"Well, for starters how about you tell me why you pushed me away? I deserved better than that, don't you think? I am your dad!"

Kellen let the blood boil to the surface. "First off, quit saying you're my dad because you never did a damn thing for me. Second, I pushed you away because I was tired of bailing your sorry ass out of jail. And third, don't you ever touch my dog again!"

"Not your dad? I fed you and kept a roof over your head, what do you call that?"

"You fed me? Is that what you call telling me to get my 'lazy ass' to the store if I was hungry? You have a warped sense of parenting."

"You are just like your mother. A mouthy, good for nothing little—"

Kellen jumped to her feet and lunged towards Jeff. "You leave my mother out of this, you bastard!"

Jeff punched a fist into the center of Kellen's chest and shoved her back down to the couch. She gasped and immediately brought her good hand and arm up across her sternum.

It was killing Joshlyn to watch all this take place. She wanted to interject, but had no idea what to say. When Jeff shoved Kellen back down to the couch, she jumped up and moved over next to her. Laying a hand on Kellen's arm, she smoothed her hair back. "You keep your hands off her!"

"Awww, isn't that sweet." Jeff started laughing and then stopped abruptly. "Don't you tell me what to do, lady, because you have no idea who I am or what I'm capable of doing."

"Oh, I know exactly who you are so don't kid yourself. Matter of fact, everybody knows who you are…or should I say aren't?"

Jeff approached her and stuck the gun in her face. "You shut your filthy mouth unless you want me to shut it for you." He waited until Joshlyn lowered her eyes and then turned back to Kellen. "Now, what you're going to do is get me some money and if I think it's enough then I'll move on. If not, well, you'll just have to see."

"And what keeps you coming back time and time again, huh?" Kellen rasped. It was hard to take a full breath at this point. Her chest was on fire.

"I guess you'll just have to take my word for it, won't you?"

The ringing of the doorbell stopped Kellen from responding. She glanced at Joshlyn and then at Jeff. He was trying to glance out a living room window to see who it was.

"Who are you expecting?"

Kellen squeezed Joshlyn's hand. "No one. We were just having a quiet morning until you showed up."

"Answer the door then and make them go away." He grabbed Joshlyn and held her in front of him. He raised the gun to her neck and smiled. "If they don't go away, she's dead."

Kellen scrambled painfully to her feet and went to the door. She took a breath, licked her lips, and opened it.

"Hi, I'm Sydney, I'm—"

Kellen interrupted before Sydney could say anything more. "I'm sorry; you must have the wrong house."

Sydney looked down at the paper in her hand and repeated the address. "Is that not where I'm at?" she said, glancing back at the numbers on the house.

"Yes, that's this address, but you must be mistaken."

Sydney watched as Kellen's eyes darted from her to some place off to her left. There was a sheen of perspiration on the woman's forehead and the pulse in her neck was very erratic. "Hm, my mistake then; I'm sorry to have bothered you."

"No problem. I hope you find who you're looking for," Kellen said as she closed the door slowly. *Please, please let her know that something isn't right!*

"Very nice, *daughter*, now sit down!" Jeff sneered.

❧ ❧ ❧ ❧

Sydney went back to her car and sat there for a minute. She knew this was the right house because Joshlyn had repeated the address twice. Even if it were the wrong house, the way the woman was acting would have raised some suspicions for her anyhow. She started the car and backed out of the driveway. She pulled down the street out of sight and pulled over to the curb. Something definitely was not right and she wasn't taking any chances. Pulling out her cell phone, she called 911. After explaining who she was, they agreed to send a couple cars her direction to check in on the owner of the home. Sydney pushed the disconnect button and tapped the phone against her chin. Even with the police on their way, she didn't feel comfortable. She got out, locked her door, and closed it. She could easily access a back alley so she walked between the houses and worked her way back down to the house. A large privacy fence surrounded the yard so Sydney went down and around the garage to where a gate allowed access. She quietly opened the fence and left it ajar…just in case. Placing one foot in front of the other, she climbed the three steps to the deck and made her way slowly across it without making herself visible through the sliding glass door. She leaned back against the house, pulled her weapon out, and slid closer to the door. As soundlessly as she could, she tried the handle to see if it was locked. It wasn't so she pushed it open just a little so she could hear what was going on inside. She really wasn't able to make out anything that was being said, but could hear a man yelling and a woman responding. Waiting for backup was the smart thing to do so she'd wait unless things escalated and she couldn't. *What the hell is going on?*

❧❧❧❧

The solitary figure knew there wasn't much longer. Hate had a way of making you do things and there was no way this hatred would be corralled. It was just a matter of time…like a ticking time bomb. If ever there was a time for action, it was now. Long enough had gone by and opportunity presented itself. He had to be stopped. Walking up the driveway and closer to the front door wasn't the hard part. The hand reached out but couldn't bring itself to ring the bell for it was shaking far too much. After a few deep breaths, it reached out again and this time made contact. Now it was just a matter of waiting.

❧ ❧ ❧ ❧

The doorbell rang again and Kellen jerked her head towards Joshlyn. She shook her head and sat still.

"Who now?" Jeff bellowed. "For someone who wasn't expecting anyone you sure have a lot of company."

"We weren't expecting anyone, that's the truth."

"I'm tired of the bullshit, little girl. Get rid of them or I will." He shook his weapon at her.

Kellen stood once again and headed to the door. This time there was no delay in her response. She swung the door open. Now she was really confused. "Yes, may I help you?" The woman looked vaguely familiar but Kellen could not place her.

"Kellen?" the woman whispered.

Kellen would recognize that voice anywhere. She grabbed the doorframe because she felt like she might faint. A wave of dizziness enveloped her and her legs felt like they might give away at any minute. "M…Mother?"

Joshlyn covered her mouth, trying to hide the gasp. She wanted to run to Kellen and be there for her because at this moment she looked like she was about to pass out. She glanced at Jeff and he had gone a little pale as well, but immediately recovered.

Jeff walked briskly to the door and pointed the

weapon at Anne. "You might as well come on in since you are just as responsible as your good for nothing daughter."

Kellen couldn't move. Her legs felt frozen to the ground. The resemblance between them was more than enough for her to know this really was her mother. She'd have stood there a lot longer if Jeff hadn't grabbed her arm and jerked her back towards the living room.

"I said, get back over there."

Kellen sat next to Joshlyn and her mother sat in the chair. The three of them just kept looking at each other. Joshlyn lightly squeezed Kellen's hand for reassurance and when she looked at her, she smiled as well. Kellen gave a slight smile then looked back at her mom.

"Well, isn't this all just sweet and cozy."

Anne slid forward in her seat a little and gestured with her hands. "Please Jeff, put the gun down and let's just talk. You don't have to do this."

"What the hell do you know, *Anne*," he emphasized with sarcasm. "You left, remember?"

"I didn't leave willingly, Jeff. You made me leave."

"You had a choice and you chose to leave!"

"How is that a choice? You threatened to hurt Kellen if I didn't just leave and disappear. It was the last thing I ever wanted to do. You never loved her so why, why would you do that?"

Jeff looked at Kellen's startled face and smirked. "Because you wanted her, that's why. If you couldn't love me anymore then you wouldn't love anybody. You got that?"

"Just because I left doesn't mean I didn't or don't

love her, Jeff. You are mistaken if you think that just because I left I quit caring."

"Then why couldn't you love me, huh? I told you I was sorry and for years, I tried to make it up to you. Wasn't that enough?"

"It might have been enough if it were the truth, Jeff." Anne glanced at Kellen with sympathy. She didn't want to hurt her any more than she already knew this was hurting, but it was time the truth came out. "You cheating with Wanda was bad enough but to find out that it didn't stop and you sired a child with her was more than I could bear."

Kellen's eyes were now wide open. It was all making sense now. That had to be the reason that Billy hated her because he was actually her half brother. Now she just felt sick and really wished she could either throw up or pass out.

"At least she loved me…or at least she did until that bitch there got involved." Jeff was pointing his weapon at Kellen and scowling. "It was all her fault that everybody who meant anything to me left."

"What…why is it my fault?" Kellen couldn't understand his reasoning. To her knowledge, she had never done anything to Wanda and was too young to remember any of it anyhow.

"Because of you, Wanda decided that I wasn't stable and that she couldn't handle it anymore. Plus Billy decided to take matters into his own hands."

"Because of me?" Kellen's voice raised. "What happened is your own damn fault for being a lousy drunk who only cared about himself! I didn't tell you to get into a fight with Bill, which by the way, did he know that Billy wasn't his?"

"What in the hell do you think that fight was

all about? Why do you think that piece of shit killed himself? Hell, he wasn't even strong enough to ignore the whispers and the finger pointing."

Chigger slowly made his way back out from the bedroom and cowered in the corner where he could still see Kellen.

"You are a real piece of work," Kellen taunted. "Not only did you lie to my mother, but you also ruined another man's life because that's just what you do!"

Jeff grabbed her by the front of the shirt and jerked her up to his face. "Don't. Push. Me. Little. Girl. I got nothing to lose!"

"Do what you're going to do, Jeff, because I'm not giving you a dime!"

He shoved her back and raised a hand to slap her. Chigger darted out at him and started growling and barking.

Jeff raised the gun in Chigger's direction and just as he pulled the trigger, Kellen lunged at him.

Chapter Twenty-three

Sydney heard the gunshot and slammed the sliding glass door open. She moved through the kitchen at a fast yet calculated pace and took an open stance in the living room.

"Freeze, FBI!"

Jeff rolled from his spot on the floor and brought the gun up in Sydney's direction. Before he could get a shot off, she fired first. The bullet caught Jeff straight between the eyes and he hit the ground.

Sydney walked over and kicked the gun away from Jeff's hand. She knelt down and felt for a pulse, knowing there wouldn't be one.

Joshlyn and Anne went over to help Kellen sit up. "Honey, are you okay?"

Kellen groaned but looked at Joshlyn. "Did you get the number of that bus that hit me?"

Joshlyn chuckled. She glanced up into the eyes that were so much like Kellen's and nodded. "Hi, I'm Joshlyn," she said, extending her hand.

Anne smiled. "Hi, Joshlyn, I'm Anne."

Joshlyn took in Kellen's position before sliding a hand up under her arm. "What say we get you off this floor, huh?" Anne put a hand under her other arm and they both helped Kellen to her feet.

"Can I get anything?"

"How about a glass of water, Syd."

Sydney acknowledged with a nod of her head

and disappeared into the kitchen. Kellen took a seat on the couch and blew a puff of air up through her bangs. "Wow, what a craptastic day!"

Joshlyn laughed and sat down beside her. "You aren't kidding!"

Sydney returned with the glass of water and handed it to Joshlyn. "Are you ok, Joshlyn?"

"Me? Oh yeah, I'm fine. It's tough stuff here who took the brunt of it all." Kellen grinned but didn't respond.

There was a knock at the front door and Sydney got up to answer it.

"Good grief, who *else* could possibly be here next?" Kellen was exasperated and way beyond all the crap going on. She was ready for it to be over…well, all except for the fact that her mother was sitting in her living room. *My mother?*

Sydney opened the door to two uniformed police officers. "Well, I'm glad you boys could be so prompt and all."

"Sorry ma'am, we were told that it wasn't an emergency."

"Yeah, I could see how, 'I'm concerned a woman is being held against her will' would not seem like an emergency," Sydney grumbled. She walked over to where the other three were sitting. "I'll be back in just a minute. I'm going to brief these guys on what happened and get a truck down here to remove the body. When that's done, we need to talk, Joshlyn."

"Ok, we'll be right here."

After Sydney left the room, Joshlyn turned back to Kellen. "Now, how are you really feeling?"

"I'm all right, Josh. None worse for the wear after all we've been through." Kellen wasn't really sure what else to say. She didn't hurt any more than she already was, although hitting the floor didn't feel very good.

"Kellen, may I ask what happened to you?" Anne asked.

"I was in a car accident," Kellen started, but stopped. Staring at Anne, she realized she knew absolutely nothing about her. She remembered bits and pieces from her childhood, but the only thing that stood out was the one evening when dinner had not been ready. "I don't know if you remember Mason or not, but he taught me how to drive. I drive race cars."

"You might actually be surprised to know that I've kept tabs on you. I know that you drive cars and I also know that you are very good. I know that you own your own business, I know about your friend Kerri, and I also know that you've been seeing Joshlyn. What I don't know is how you feel about knowing that I am alive. I know it's a shock, Kellen, but I swear I wouldn't have done it if he hadn't threatened your life."

"What happened, because I really don't understand how all this came about."

They stopped talking for a bit when two men came in to remove Jeff's body from the room. Kellen looked away as he was wheeled out.

Anne placed a hand on Kellen's arm. "None of this was your fault. I caught Jeff with Wanda and he promised it wouldn't happen again. That lasted maybe a month and then they were back at it. The final straw was when I found out that Wanda was carrying his child. I didn't find this out immediately though. It wasn't until I saw Bill out one night and we were talking when he mentioned how ecstatic he was about the baby. He said they had been trying for years and was finally told he was sterile. I put two and two together and when Billy Jr. was born, I did something I shouldn't have and looked at the records. Being a nurse, I had access to them and Billy's blood type did not match Wanda's or Bill's, however it did match Jeff's. I confronted Jeff about it and he became furious over it. He told me to leave and never come back. When I said fine and started packing our stuff, he said that I could not take you with me. He threatened to hunt me down and kill you if I did. So I did the only thing I knew how to do to keep you safe."

"What about after he went to jail? Why didn't you come to me then?"

"I went to him at the prison once he was incarcerated. He told me he had people on the outside that were keeping tabs on me and that he would know if I made any attempt to come back into your life. I couldn't take that chance, Kellen."

Kellen stared at her mother and couldn't decide how to feel about it all. Before she could ask another question, Anne continued talking.

"It wasn't too long ago that I realized his 'people' on the outside was just Billy. Once I found this out I didn't hesitate any longer. I was just waiting for the right moment to get in contact with you."

"I am so sorry," Kellen whispered.

Anne leaned a little closer and leaned down so Kellen had to look her in the eye. "I never stopped loving you, Kel."

Tears immediately sprung to Kellen's eyes. It had been so long since she heard that name come out of her mother's mouth and the ache in her chest was overwhelming. She tried to hold back the sob that was threatening to spill out, but she couldn't contain it. She starting crying and didn't feel like she'd be able to stop.

Anne looked at Joshlyn. She wasn't sure what to do. Joshlyn nodded her head towards Kellen and mouthed, "Go on."

Anne pulled Kellen to her and held her. The sobs continued and Anne whispered consoling words into Kellen's hair. "It's all going to be okay, Kellen. I love you and I'm never leaving again. I'm here for you." Anne stopped breathing when Kellen's arm circled her and hung on tight.

Joshlyn stood up and quietly left the room. She wanted to give mom and daughter a chance to talk and bond. She stepped out onto the front porch as Sydney made her way back up the driveway.

Sydney stopped in front of Joshlyn. "Wow, what a day. Do you always like to have this much fun?"

"It has been a rather interesting past few weeks, I'll give you that. I'm glad you were here, Syd. I'm so sorry I didn't call you sooner."

"I'd like to say I should have come sooner, but if I had I wouldn't have been here for today so it all worked out for the best."

"What did you need to talk to me about?"

"Here, have a seat on the step." Sydney sat down and waited for Joshlyn to do the same. "We found the other brother. I was trying to contact you to tell you that you might have to come back for a trial, but he was murdered in prison. There was an investigation, but nothing came of it. Essentially hon, you are in the clear. They are all gone now."

"No more hiding? No more looking over my shoulder?"

"Nope. Which is a good thing since I see you aren't wearing your contacts." Sydney grinned.

"Mmm, yeah, well, Kellen really likes me without the contacts." Joshlyn blushed.

"I just bet she does," Sydney teased. "Seriously though, you look happy."

"I am, Syd, I really am. She's the one."

"Ahh, I am so happy for you. You deserve this more than anyone I know."

"I had long since lost hope of it ever happening. I just accepted that this is the way life is supposed to be and that was that."

"So what changed your mind?"

"Do you even have to ask? You've seen my girlfriend, right?" Joshlyn laughed.

"She is a pretty hot little number."

They laughed together for a minute before Joshlyn continued. "Really though, she was under my skin before I had a chance to put up any barriers. If I'm being honest though, I didn't and wouldn't have fought too hard against them. I about ruined it though."

"How so?"

"When Kellen won a race awhile back it made some national headlines and somebody I know saw me in the interview. I freaked out, said some really awful things to Kellen, and then broke up with her."

Sydney just stared at Joshlyn with a slack jaw. "I wish you had returned my calls because I could have at least alleviated that fear for you."

"I know, I know." Joshlyn sighed. "I was scared, Syd. My mind conjured up all these things you could have been calling me about and they were, of course, the worst possible scenarios."

"Well, at least it all worked out okay. Kellen doing all right?"

"I think she will be. It's been a big shock for her what with her mother showing up. All this time she thought she had died."

"Damn, that poor woman has been put through the ringer."

"You know something? You're right and I think it's time she gets a little rest and relaxation."

"Uh oh, I hear some major planning in your near future."

"You got it! C'mon, let's head back inside and I will give you a formal introduction."

"Before we go, I wanted to give you this. It was in Jeff's pocket." She handed a picture to Joshlyn.

Joshlyn took the picture in her hand and uncurled the edges on it. It was an older picture of Kellen and she had a gorgeous smile on her face. "Thanks, I'm not sure I should give her this. It might creep her out to know he was carrying it around. Don't mention it to her, okay?"

"Good idea and my lips are sealed."

Joshlyn hooked her arm through Syd's and pulled her to the house.

Chapter Twenty-four

Kellen rubbed her thumb across Joshlyn's and rolled her head to the side. "Are you going to tell me where we're going?"

"You will just have to wait and see, my love. I promise you won't be disappointed though."

"Promises, promises."

They were finally headed out on the vacation that Joshlyn worked tirelessly to plan. If anyone deserved a much-needed vacation, it was Kellen. In the last two months, all the details finally wrapped themselves up. Kellen found out that her mom had been sending the threatening letters. Her hopes were that Kellen would get nervous or afraid and go to the police about it, thus forcing them to give her some type of protective custody. Anne knew that Jeff was due to get out of jail and knowing how vindictive he was made her afraid for Kellen's safety. The authorities had picked Billy up after Kellen told them what Jeff had said about him taking matters into his own hands. After hours and hours of interrogation, Billy finally admitted that he tried to kill Kellen during the race and that the accident long ago with Peetie was meant for her. He found out that Kellen was his half sister and hated her for it. Everything was always about her and he blamed her for never having a father figure in his life. Billy went on to say that he was in the truck the day Bill Sr. had killed himself. Billy told Bill over and over what a worthless piece of shit he was and kept goading him to just pull the trigger…to be a real man for once and do it. In the end, Bill did do it and Billy walked away. No angrier, yet no happier either.

Bob and the crew were busy building another car for Kellen. She'd told them emphatically that she wanted to race again and was more than ready. It made Joshlyn nervous, but she wasn't about to ask Kellen to stop doing something she loved. Plus, this was the first major accident Kellen had ever had and at that, it was a planned accident. Kellen needed to be doing the things she loved.

Kellen had Joshlyn over one night for dinner specifically so they could each get rid of the things in their lives that they felt either held them back or were no longer needed.

Kellen thought back to the night and how rewarding it felt.

"You have everything you need?" Joshlyn asked.

"Yep, let's go out to the fire pit. It should be good and ready by now."

They went out the sliding door and waited for Chigger to follow them. They both sat in a chair and Chigger lay down between Kellen's feet.

Joshlyn wanted to go first so she opened the tattered brown box. She pulled all the old newspaper articles out and held them in her hand. "Are you sure you don't want to read any of these?"

"I'm positive, Josh. What you told me was more than enough. I don't want all the gritty details. I'm just happy it's all over for you."

"Good enough for me." She tossed all the articles in the fire and watched them burn to ashes and disappear. The next thing she pulled from the box were

some pictures. She's already shown them to Kellen. There were a couple pictures of her mom, her sisters, and some of the people she thought were here friends. She tossed those into the fire as well. The only ones she kept were the ones of her friend, Lori, who stood by her. The final thing to go into the flames was the brown box itself. She was more than happy to see it go because for almost three years it alone was the most constant reminder of everything she'd lost.

When Joshlyn was finished, Kellen took the stack of stuff she brought out and held it in one hand. She had a bunch of pictures of Jeff, Jeff and Anne, and a few of Jeff and Kellen. He represented a part of her life that she was choosing to let go. She tossed the pictures into the fire and then unfolded the articles about Peetie's death. They too landed in the fire on top of the pictures. The last thing to go were several recent articles about the wreck at the track, the shooting of Jeff by an FBI agent, and articles about Billy and everything he confessed.

Joshlyn and Kellen both sat stoically watching the fire consume the items until there was nothing left but ashes.

"Hey, did you call your mom before we left?"

Kellen opened her eyes and smiled. "Yep, I told her how long we'd be gone and that maybe when we got back she could come over for dinner one night." Anne knew that Kellen needed to take things slow but was happy that Kellen at least wanted her in her life. Despite all that had happened, Kellen understood that it wasn't really Anne's fault that she wasn't around. Life was too short to hold a grudge about something that couldn't be helped. Bottom line is that she wanted her mother in her life and wanted to get to know her. "I meant to ask if you had decided to give Lori a call or not."

"I think I will, but after we get back. I know this will be hard on her and I really don't want anything any more emotional than you and I right now."

"I completely understand," Kellen said with a wink. "How much longer till we get there anyhow?"

"We are almost there, you big baby!"

Kellen laughed. "Hey, my butt is just getting numb." She scratched at her left wrist and glanced at it again. The cast had finally come off and the skin still felt really dry. She was constantly rubbing lotion into it. The muscle hadn't lost much tone, but it still looked a little punier than her right. Her stitches had also been removed awhile back and she had a nice little pink scar. The hair through her eyebrow hadn't grown back and at this point, it probably wouldn't, but that was ok. It made her look distinctive…at least that's what Joshlyn told her. Thankfully, it wasn't a large area that was missing, just a small line through the middle.

Kellen sat up in her seat when Joshlyn turned off onto a gravel road. They drove quite a ways on the gravel road until they pulled into a wooded area. At the cross section in the road, Joshlyn made a left and pulled up to a cabin.

"Hang on, I'll be right back."

Joshlyn hopped out and Kellen looked all around. There were trees among trees and more trees. She could see a road that led further on down, but past that all you could see were more trees. "Where do you think we are, huh, Chigger?" Chigger whined, but his tail wagged back and forth, making his whole body shake. Kellen laughed and scratched him under the chin as Joshlyn came back out and got back into the

SUV.

"All right, we are down there, last cabin on the right."

"Uh, Josh, all I see down there are trees."

Joshlyn grinned. "Just wait, you'll see."

They drove down through the trees and the further back they got Kellen could see cabins. All the cabins had trees enclosing them so you couldn't see the cabin next to you. They pulled all the way to the end and turned into a drive. The drive went through the trees and down a little bit. Kellen could see a lake out behind the cabin and trees lining the lake all around.

"C'mon, we'll come back for the bags in a bit. I want to show you something before it gets much darker."

Kellen stepped out of the truck, opened the passenger door to let Chigger out, and walked to the front where Joshlyn took her hand. They walked down the cobbled stones and onto the front porch of the cabin. Once there, they followed the wrap-around porch to the back where a small deck with a grill and built in deck seating came into view. The best part, though, was the ramp that led from the deck down to a big dock that jetted out into the water and overlooked the lake.

"This is absolutely gorgeous, Josh."

Joshlyn pulled her down the ramp and onto the dock. "Have a seat." Joshlyn sat down with her legs hanging over the edge.

Kellen sat down beside her and wrapped an arm over her shoulders. Joshlyn leaned into her shoulder and wrapped her arm around Kellen's waist. Chigger plopped down behind them and sniffed the air before laying his head down and sighing.

They sat there quietly while the sun set over the lake. The frogs were croaking and the crickets were chirping. The water looked like glass it was so still. A bird took flight from a tree and Kellen turned to look at Joshlyn. She leaned in and kissed her with more emotion than she'd ever felt in her entire life. Desire was one thing, but this…this was different.

"Like a moth to a flame, like a song without a name, I've never been the same since I met you," Kellen quoted softly.

"Eric Clapton?"

"Mmhmm…but it's true. You turned my world upside down, Josh."

"And you turned my world right side up. I love you, Kellen."

"And I love you, honey."

About the Author

Tara lives in Missouri with her partner of 16 years. She has been in the medical field for 25 years and enjoys it immensely. When not working or writing, Tara likes to spend her time reading, dabbling with photography, watching sports on TV (Go Royals!!!) or catching up with her favorite shows (Chicago Fire, Chicago PD and Stalker.) Her first novel, Traffic Stop, was a GCLS Debut Author finalist.

Feel free to contact Tara any time via Facebook

https://www.facebook.com/tara.wentz.54

or email- twentz67@yahoo.com

Other titles available at Sapphire Books

The Demon Within - ISBN - 978-1-939062-81-9

What do you do when you're a demon hunter who is also possessed by an ancient demon who needs to feed off other demonic spirits? Where do you turn when that demon's hunger for the deaths of others reaches its apex causing you to become an overzealous killer and murderer of evil? How do you live with yourself night after night as you wade through the detritus that was once a demonic entity destroying human lives? And who can you turn to when your very humanity starts slipping through your fingers....

Forever Faithful ISBN - 978-1-939062-75-8

Life is what happens when you make other plans, and Nic and Claire have just found out that life and the Marine Corps have other plans for their lives.

Nic Caldwell has served her country, met the woman of her dreams, and has reached the rank of Lieutenant Colonel. She's studying at one of the nation's most prestigious military universities, setting her sights on a research position after graduation. Things couldn't be better and then it happens; a sudden assignment to Afghanistan derails any thoughts of marriage and wedded bliss. Another combat zone, another tragedy, and Nic suddenly finds herself fighting for her life....

After Shadow - ISBN - 978-1-939062-10-9

Clara always knew she was different, but just how different she was was to be seen. She will be forced on a journey to places that, though nightmarish to some, make perfect sense to her. While living a life in darkness and shadow, massaging the ghosts we all want to hide from beneath the covers, she will discover her own light of day. But, can she discover her heart?

The Purveyor - ISBN – 978-1-939062-65-9

After theater professor Adair Wilson unwittingly assists in the abduction of two Pittock students, she sets out on a death-defying quest to rescue the twin girls whose rare anatomical quirk makes them a target for paparazzi and fetishists.

When Adair's wealthy family refuses to help and the girls' family denies their existence, Adair must battle an underground prostitution ring protected by corrupt police.

With only her lover, Helen Ivers, at her side, Adair turns a handful of clues into a plan of action that pits her against the world's most ruthless human trafficker, a woman known only as the Purveyor.

Love Sucks ISBN - 978-1-939062-50-5

Tragedy and heartbreak drive Dana McComb to a Caribbean island where she sets about to becoming a hermit. Settling into numbness seems to be the only way to suppress the psychic visions that once showed her the death of her soul mate. A failed rebound relationship leaves her even more intent on losing herself in the loneliness of her isolated house on the hill....

Deep Merge - ISBN – 978-1-939062-52-9

Kaesah, a geneticist from an all female species living on the other side of the galaxy, is stranded on Earth due to the death of her mate who was vital in piloting their starship. Kaesah must report the disturbing events on Earth that could impact the survival of her species. To reach her world, Kaesah has no choice but to find a human woman capable of Deep Merge, a process required to guide her ship through the galaxy. Can Kaesah overcome her aversion to humans to form a harmonious bond with one?